PRAISE FOR DOUGLAS CLEGG'S
FICTION

"Clegg's stories can chill the spine so effectively
that the reader should keep paramedics on
standby."
—Dean Koontz, *New York Times* bestselling
author.

"Douglas Clegg has become the new star in horror
fiction."
—Peter Straub, *New York Times* bestselling author
of *Ghost Story* and, with Stephen King, *The
Talisman*

"Douglas Clegg is the best horror novelist of the
post-Stephen King generation."
— Bentley Little, bestselling author

"Clegg gets high marks on the terror scale…"
—*The Daily News* (New York)

CONTENTS

THE WORDS

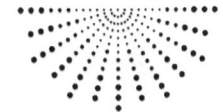

DOUGLAS CLEGG

ALKEMARA
PRESS

For permissions contact: DClegg@DouglasClegg.com

Cover art provided by Damonza.com

ISBN-13: 978-1-944668-34-1

ISBN-10: 1-944668-34-9

Disclaimer:

The Words is a work of fiction. Names, places, characters and
incidents are a product of the author's imagination. Any
resemblance to actual locales, events, or persons, living or dead,
is entirely coincidental.

Purity

The Words

SERIES

THE HARROW SERIES

Nightmare House, Book 1

Mischief, Book 2

The Infinite, Book 3

The Abandoned, Book 4

The Necromancer (Prequel Novella)

Isis

THE CRIMINALLY INSANE SERIES

Bad Karma, Book 1

Red Angel, Book 2

Night Cage, Book 3

THE VAMPYRICON TRILOGY

The Priest of Blood, Book 1

The Lady of Serpents, Book 2

The Queen of Wolves, Book 3

THE CHRONICLES OF MORDRED

Mordred, Bastard Son (Book 1)

COLLECTIONS

Lights Out: Collected Stories

Night Asylum

The Nightmare Chronicles

Wild Things

The Poisoner's Garden & Others

BOX SET BUNDLES

Bad Places (3 Novels)

Coming of Age (3 Dark Novellas)

Dark Rooms (3 Novels)

Criminally Insane: The Series (3 Novels)

Halloween Chillers

Harrow: Three Novels (Books 1-3)

Harrow: Four Novels (Books 1-4)

Haunts (8 Novel Box Set)

Lights Out (3 Collection Box Set)

Night Towns (3 Novels)

The Vampyricon Trilogy (3 Novels)

With more new novels & stories to come.

THE WORDS

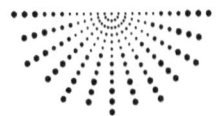

THE END IS LIKE THIS

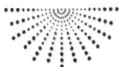

After the last match goes out, he mouths the words to the Our Father, but it brings him no comfort.

He remembers the Veil.

He remembers the way things moved and how the sky looked under its influence.

He doubts now that a prayer could be answered. He doubts everything he has come to believe about the world.

The echo of the last scream. He can hear it, even though the room is silent. It seems to be in his head now: the final cry.

Hope it's final.

The scream is too seductive, he knows. He understands what's out there.

It's attracted to noise, because it doesn't see with its eyes anymore. It sees by smell and sound and vibration.

He has begun to think of it by its new name,

only he doesn't want to ever say that name out loud. Again.

Your flesh won't forget.

Prickly feeling along the backs of his hands, along his calves. In his mind, he goes through the alphabet, trying to latch onto something he can work around. Something that will give him a jump into remembering the words.

He presses himself against the wall as if it will hide him.

Rough stone. No light. Need light. Damn.

He thinks he must be delirious because the goofiest things go through his mind: Michelle's phrase, *Unfrigginlikely, Spaceman Mark.*

Those aren't the words. Spaceman Mark. Hey, Space! What planet you on today? Planet Dark, that's what I'm on. Planet Midnight.

And out of matches.

The wind dies, momentarily, beyond the cracked window.

The damn ticking of the watch.

Someone's heartbeat.

The sensation of freezing and burning alternately — a fever.

The sticky feeling under his armpits.

The rough feeling of his tongue against the roof of his mouth.

The interminable waiting.

Seconds that become hours in his mind. In those seconds, he is running through sounds in his head — the words? What are they? Laiya-oauwraii...no.

That's the beginning of the name. Don't say it again. It might call it right to you. You might make it stronger. For all you know. What the hell are the words?

He clutches the carved bone in his left hand. It's smooth in his fist. Like ivory, a tusk from some fallen beast. Slight ridges where the words are carved. Like trying to read Braille.

If only I could read them. Need to get light. Some light.

Distracted by the smell.

That would be the first one it got.

Over in the corner, something moves. Darkness against darkness.

Someone he can't see in the dark is over there.

Eyesight is failure, Dash once told him. Perception is failure. All that there is, all that there ever will be, cannot be perceived in the light of day. At night, the only perceptions turn inward.

The words? The words. Maybe if you remember them, you can stop it. Maybe it reverses. Or maybe if you just say them…

Moves his lips, trying to form vowel sounds.

The dry taste. Humid and weather-scorned all around.

In his throat, a desert.

Every word he has ever heard in his life spins through his mind. But not the words he needs.

Not the ones he wants to remember tonight.

A beautiful night. Dark. No light whatsoever but the ambient light of the world itself.

Summer. Humid. Post-storm. One of those rich storms that sweeps the sky with crackling blue and white lightning, and the roars of lions. But the storm has passed — and that curious wet silence remains.

Taste of brine in the air from the water, a few miles away.

He remembers summer storms like this — their majesty as they wash the June sky clean, bringing a gloom on their caped shoulders, but leaving behind not a trace of it. The smell of oak and beech and cedar and salt and the murky stink of the ponds and bogs. Their years together, all in those smells. All in the dark.

The night, summer, perhaps just a few hours before the sun might rise.

Might.

He wonders if he'll ever see another storm. Another summer.

Another dawn.

Those damn words.

"Your flesh will remember the name even if your mind forgets," Dash had told him, and he had still thought it was a game when Dash had said it. "The name gets in your bones and in your heart. Just by hearing it once. But the words are harder to remember. They don't want you to know the words because it binds them. So, listen very carefully. Listen. Each time I say them, repeat them exactly back to me."

He's shivering. Sweating. Nausea and dizziness

both within him, the pit of his stomach. Something's scratchy around his balls — feels like a mosquito buzzing all along the inside of his legs. Twitching in his fingers. Tensing his entire body.

Afraid to take another breath.

A conversation replays in his head:

"It's not that hard. Watch."

"I can't. I just…"

"All you do is take the thing and bring it down like this. Think of it as a game."

"I can't do it."

"Don't think of it like that. Pretend it's a game. It doesn't mean what it looks like. You've been trained to think this is bad by church and school and your parents. And the world outside. But it is not real. It is just a game, only nobody else knows this. They're stupid. Nobody's going to get hurt. Least of all one of us. Least of all you or me. I would never let it happen. You're like my brother."

"I know. But I can't."

"All right. I'll do it. I'll just do it. Just remember what you're supposed to do. As soon as it happens. As soon as my eyes close. Promise? Okay?"

"Okay, okay."

"And the words. After. If it's too much. You know what to say. You remember?"

"Yes."

"You know how to pronounce them? You have to know. If this gets out of hand, you can stop it.

The name for me, and the words to stop it. If it's too awful."

"I know, I know."

"Because it might get too awful. I don't know."

"Sure. Of course. I remember how to say them."

"And the name?"

He has no problem remembering the name. He'd like to blot it out of his mind. The name is on the tip of his tongue, and he can't seem to forget how to say it, how to pronounce it perfectly. The words have somehow vanished from his mind.

He tries to remember the words, now. How they sound. The language was foreign, but he couldn't read them off the bone. Especially with no light. But even if he had some light, he knew the letters looked like scribbles and symbols. They didn't look like sounds. All he can remember is the name, and he doesn't want to remember that.

A name like that shouldn't be said in a church.

A New England church. *Saint Something. Old Something Church. Older than old, perhaps.* Nearly a crypt. Made of slate and stone. Puritanical and lovely and a bit like a prison, now. Church of punishment. Rocky churchyard behind it.

He remembers the graves with the mud and the high grasses and the smell of wild onion and lavender, as if it were years ago rather than the past hour. Smell of summer, wet grass, and that fertile, splendid odor of new leaves, new blossoms.

The smell of life.

He is inside the church. In a room. The altar is at the opposite end.

Danny had the lighter, he thinks.

If I get it, maybe I can at least save her.

He wasn't sure if the shape in the doorway was Danny, or the thing that he didn't even want to name. Not Dash. Not anyone he had ever met or known.

An 'It'. A Thing. A Creature. Something without a Name.

But it has a name. He knows the name, but he does not intend to ever say it again. He knows the name too well, but it's the words he keeps trying to remember. The ones that are on the bone. The words that might stop it from continuing.

He tries to lick his lips, but it's no use. His mouth is dry.

Dry from too much screaming.

Nearby, there's a very slight noise. A sliver of a noise. He is sensitive to sound.

In the Nowhere.

Someone might've just died outside. He doesn't know for sure. Who? He just heard the last of someone's life in a slight moaning sound.

The open window. No breeze.

Just that sound.

A soft but unpleasant *ohhhhhh*.

The puppy whimpers. Somewhere nearby.

Other sounds, barely audible, seem huge.

Branches against the rooftop. Scraping lightly.

His heartbeat. A rapping hammer.

In the dark, the ticking of his watch is too loud. He slowly draws it from his wrist. Carefully, he presses it down into the left-hand pocket of his jeans. The watch clinks slightly against his keys. He holds his breath.

Needs to cough.

Fight it. Fight it. Swallow the cough. Don't let it out.

Closes his eyes, against the darkness. Closes his eyes to block it out. To make it go away.

Holds his breath for another count. The cough is gone.

Brief sound.

Someone's breathing. Over there. Across the room. Small room. More than closet, less than room.

Her? Thank god. Thank god. He licks his lips. Mouth, dry.

After a few minutes, he can just make out her shape.

He's staring at her, and she's staring at him, but they can't really see each other. Just forms in the dark. Michelle? Ambient light from beneath cracks in the walls creates a barely visible aura around her as he stares.

Dead of night. Dread of night.

The dread comes after the knowledge. He

remembers the line from the book. That awful book that he thought was fiction.

But the words do not come to him. The sounds of them, just beyond his memory.

Breathing hard, but as quietly as he can.

Smells his own breath. The stink of his under-arms. Glaze of sweat covering his body. Shirt plastered to him. Hair wet and greasy against his scalp.

The chill that hasn't left him, not since he came up out of the earth. Burning chill.

She's going to do it.

Or I am.

One of them is going to scream again. He knows it. He wasn't even sure if he had stopped screaming a half hour before.

Problem is, when the screaming starts, it happens.

And neither of them wants it to happen.

But the puppy is okay.

It doesn't want the puppy.

That's what someone said before. How many minutes ago? Did he say it? Had he said it and just not remembered it? "It doesn't want the puppy."

She whispers something. Or else he imagines she whispers.

Or it's the sound of the leaves on the trees, brushing the rooftop.

If it's her, it's wrong for her to whisper. Neither of them knows what decibel level it needs to find them, but she whispers anyway, "Please say it's a game. Please god, say it's a game."

He's not close enough, but he wants to hold her. Hold her tight. Rewind the night back to day, back a year or more, so he can undo it all. He wants everything to turn out okay, but he knows it won't.

Most of all, he wants her to shut her mouth up. He wants to hold her and press his lips or his hand against her mouth and keep in whatever she's trying to let out.

Silence. Come on, silence. Don't...

Even her whisper is too loud.

And it hears her.

And it wants to make her scream.

IF SHE SCREAMS, it's all over.

Not just the game. The game will never be over.

If we can just hold out until daylight, he thinks.

But the noise begins. From her throat. He wants to shut her up, but he can't. He can't. She's over there in the dark, and he's on the other side of the room from her.

The scream is coming up from her lungs in a staccato gurgle.

She can't hold it in.

That's when he hears the sound.

Not her scream.

Dear Sweet Jesus, do not let that noise out of your mouth. Do not scream. It is inside here. With us.

He hears the sound it makes as it moves.

Wet, popping sounds, like bones springing free of joints, and then that stink of over ripeness.

Rotten. Steaming.

Then that awful thumping begins again.

And the steady hissing, as if dozens of snakes trail behind it.

He leans back against the wall, wanting to press himself into the wood as far as he can go. Wanting his molecules to change and move through the wood so he can just escape.

He's praying so hard he feels like his skull is going to crack open, only the prayers are all messed up and he's sure they don't work if you get them wrong. Dear God, Dear Jesus, please help this poor sinner, Hail Mary, full of grace, Hail Mary, full of grace and the fruit of thy womb, Jesus, Our Father who art in heaven, hallowed be thy name.

It whispers something in the darkness.

He begins shivering when he hears the words.

The girl in the corner finally begins to scream as if she already knows the game is up.

It sweeps toward her. *Sweeps.*

He can't stop it. He's too scared. He's so scared he's afraid he's going to pee his pants and start giggling because something inside his head is going a little haywire.

And then, he feels the wet fingers — he hopes they're fingers – along his ankles.

He tries to remain perfectly still.

Perfectly still.

Like I'm not alive.

Like I'm not even here.

Remember. Come on. Remember. Remember.

Damn it, the words.

2

BEFORE THE NIGHT

All that screaming and darkness happened one night when they were eighteen, but the truth was, it started long before, at least for Mark.

The longest day of the year; the shortest night of the year. But they didn't take off for the party until the dark had fallen. No one in his right mind went to a party early.

But that was the end of it.

The beginning was a game. A game within a game.

The game was about darkness.

THERE WAS a history of minor corruption between Mark and Dash that began when they were thirteen.

Dash was named, he told Mark early in their

friendship, for Dashiell Hammett, a writer. Dash refused to read anything Hammett had written.

Mark was called the Spaceman because, he assumed, he must've seemed spacey at times. He didn't do any illegal drugs, but other kids were sure he did. Dash only called Mark "Marco."

"Names have power," Dash told him. "Only I can call you Marco."

Back when they were a bit younger, Mark was completely unnoticeable. He had few friends, and tended to mumble in school. Like the other students at the Gardner School, he had been pulled from public school for one mysterious reason or another.

He arrived, newly thirteen, at the Gardner School in Manosset Sound, at a spur in the Massachusetts coastline. It was nearly a forty minute drive from his home, which was in an outer suburb of Boston.

Some nights, he slept over at the boarding department, but most, he went home. Sometimes, his mother or father drove him to school; sometimes he carpooled with another older student who had a car.

The Gardner School was the only school that would take him after the little incident with the knife.

"I found it out on the blacktop," he'd told the guidance counselor at his previous school. "I did not bring it to school. I didn't threaten to kill anyone. And I didn't stab him. I held it up and I wanted him to get away from me. He was a bully. He tried to push me. He got cut because he pushed me on the blacktop and then he was about to hit me and I put the knife up between us."

Dash told Mark that he was at the Gardner School for something messed up, too.

"I have an IQ of 180, so I'm apparently really smart only I'm bored with school already. Why don't they get better teachers here? It costs a fortune to go here. You'd think they could hire a better group."

They'd bonded immediately.

They both turned up in French class, sitting next to each other in eighth grade. They found themselves with lockers side by side. Mark was an altar boy at St. Peter's. As he got into his robe one Sunday, *there* was Dash inside one of the confessionals, his head poking out from behind the narrow doorway.

"Wanna smoke?"

"How'd you get out here?" Mark asked. Dash lived closer to school than to Mark's neighborhood.

"Bus."

"I didn't know you were Catholic."

"I'm not," Dash said. "I don't believe in that stuff. I was just waiting for you to get off-duty. And have a smoke. I saw you smoke in the stalls at school. I like to hang out in graveyards, and there's a nice one behind this god place. I was having a smoke, and I saw you troop in with all the other god people."

Dash had a funny rhythm to his speaking voice, even then. As if he were preparing lectures, an old professor in the body of an adolescent.

"We're too young to smoke," Mark said. "And it's bad for you."

"Like I said, I saw you smoke at school. Or at least, I thought it was you. Do you have vices? Self-destructive ones?"

Mark only hesitated a moment. He had never smoked a cigarette before in his life.

"They might catch us in there."

"Nope. Confessional's all empty. Come on," Dash said.

He held up a pack of Marlboros. "This is the slowest way of killing yourself. One cigarette at a time, but if you start young enough, it'll help."

"Not everyone dies from that," Mark said.

"Everyone dies from something. That's the problem of life. You're just going to die," Dash said. "Me, I'll get hooked on any number of things if I can. It's always good to improve the odds if you want to succeed."

"That's like suicide. That's a sin."

"For you. You're Catholic. You have that whole resurrection of the body thing and the life everlasting, choirboy," Dash said. "Not that I don't find that appealing. I'd love to die and then come back. Conquering death should be the alternate goal if dying is the common one. I'd love to be a messiah. It would suit me. Now, come on, let's have a smoke."

In school, they went into the janitor's closet -- a deep broom closet that had stacks of *Playboy*s beneath a pile of cleaning supplies. The closet stank of *Comet* and bleach and oil.

"Just shut off the lights."

"Why?"

"Just shut 'em off."

"Okay."

Off went the lights.

"Listen," Dash said.

"To what?"

"Just listen. Hear my breathing? Now?"

Mark mumbled something about bad breath.

"See? This is the Nowhere," Dash said.

"This definitely is nowhere."

"*The* Nowhere. It's a different place than when the lights are on," Dash said. "Different rules apply. Hell, there are no rules. With the light on, it's all rules and regulations and laws and order. But with the dark, it's a different world. When you're dead, you're in the dark."

"When I'm dead, I'll be somewhere else."

"You think so?" Dash asked. "Now here's the thing. I know these people who believe they talk to the dead."

"Psychics?" Mark said.

"No, none of that crap. I mean people who actually believe they talk to the dead. They summon them from graves. They believe it. I don't know if I believe it yet."

"Are they in school?"

"Don't be ridiculous. I met them in a graveyard. Manosset has more than just the rocky beach. There's the Old Church. They were there. Doing a ceremony. They were sacrificing a turtle."

"Gross."

"It wasn't as gross as you'd think," Dash said. "They told me all about the Nowhere. How it changes the world. Darkness. Night. Absence of light. And in the dark, they think they talk to the dead. They have an old religion. Older than, well, yours. One of them told me that people still practice it, only no one ever talks about it. Bands of believers, basically. It's not so much different from yours. Only, they believe in a messiah of darkness. A savior who comes by night."

"You making this up?"

"I wish I were. I don't really believe it. But they do. I find it a very attractive kind of belief system. It's this interesting idea. And you know how I like interesting ideas. And you've got this absolute connection between death and life. Bringing back the dead," Dash said this last part in full old professor mode. Then, he asked, "Do you believe in God?"

"Possibly."

"Well, then you might as well possibly believe

in the Nowhere. I mean, virgins, miracles, and raising people from the dead. It's not that far from what they believe."

"You mean your made-up people who sacrifice turtles?"

"Not just turtles," Dash said. "Other stuff, too. Goats sometimes. Chickens. I'll introduce you to them one night. Did you know that a man named Crossing actually wrote several stories about their group? More than a hundred years ago. He was one of them. People thought he was writing fiction, but apparently, none of it was made up. I'll loan you one of his books sometime. He said that the darkness has a reality to it that lets illogic through. Isn't that a cool way of saying it? The darkness lets illogic through. He called it the Veil with capital V."

He paused.

Mark was about to laugh. Was this a joke? Was he *serious*? *I mean, with a capital V? Come on.*

Mark didn't say any of this out loud.

"It's not so different than anything else, really. It's almost logical. There aren't any virgins in it. But there *are* some miracles. Take the streets: lights on. It's normal. Boring. At night? Lights out. No light. No moonlight even. It's a place where you make up the rules. You define the space. You create what's there and what's not," Dash said, his breath all warm. "You create what's there. And maybe *it* creates what's there."

"*It?*"

"The Nowhere."

"With a Capital N?"

Dash ignored this. "Believe what you want but there's something out there. In the dark. If you're in it long enough, it comes out. That's why they had to do the sacrifices. They told me it stops worse things from happening. You know about Eastern philosophy?"

Before Mark could answer, Dash kept going:

"Some of it is about how it's all an illusion. Everything we think we see. It's not what's really there. And if that's true, maybe what's really there is something else. Only we don't see it because we're too busy perceiving the crap we expect to see. We're taught from an early age to see things a certain way, and we name things so that they stay that way. But the darkness is fluid. It defies perception. You know how your eyeball works? How everything you see, you're really seeing upside-down, only your eye somehow adjusts it back again?"

Mark had never heard of this before. Sometimes, Dash's ideas went right over his head; or else they hit him square in the face and gave him massive headaches.

"Or a red rose. It's not really red. We see it because of the absence of some pigment and how all the other colors are there, and that somehow makes it red. But if you turn off the light, is the rose still red? Or is it no color? Is it even a rose? Does it become something else in the dark? And do you become something else in the dark?""

"Cool," Mark said. "But, I mean, I'm…me. I'm me even now. Even in the dark."

"Are you? Are you sure?"

Mark laughed a little.

"I'm not joking. Are you the same you in the dark as you were when the light was on?" Dash asked. "Would you do the same things in the light of day that you'd do if no one could see you? Do you ever wonder why people have sex in the dark?"

"Because they're embarrassed?" Mark said.

"Maybe it's 'because they can be something different in the dark. Or maybe they really are something different in the dark," Dash said. "Maybe right now, you're not even Mark. Maybe you're something else. Do you believe in life after death?"

"Well," Mark fumbled with his thoughts. "I'm sort of Catholic."

"Sort of?"

Mark shrugged. "I believe some things and not others."

"The only thing I believe about Christianity is the resurrection of the body," Dash said. "I mean, I think dead bodies still have somebody in them. Maybe we do them a disservice by burying them."

"What, you mean if you didn't bury a body it would just be fine?"

"Not saying that," Dash said. "If you can't

think deeper than that, Marco, I don't know about you. I just don't know. I mean, what are those caskets for? They're like little traps. What if we could all roll the stones away from our tombs after we die? Maybe there'd be more messiahs around. Who knows? Let me give you a rundown on deity.

"First, God's name is not God. Second, in the Old Testament, they called him Yahweh or Jehovah. In Greek, Deus. The Greek name for the top dog god was Zeus. Pretty close to Deus, don't you think? And Jehovah is pretty close sounding to the Roman god, Jove, alias Jupiter.

"I won't even go into what I learned about the goddess Ishtar and her relationship to your Queen of Heaven. You don't want to know what the word Easter comes from, trust me. It would blow you out of that little church world you're in. God, Yahweh, *what have you.* And none of these are the names of God, and even with God, there are other gods.

"That's why you have this commandment, 'Thou Shalt Have No Other Gods Before Me.' It's because there *are* other ones. And people can't say their names because no one really knows how to say the names. They used to. That's what priests in ancient times did. That was their power. They knew the real names of the gods. And naming them means bringing them. Invoking them.

"And that's what these people in the Nowhere have. For centuries, they've kept alive the name of a particular god. Maybe it's 'the' God. I don't know. But the name of the god is the power. And the god of the Nowhere is all about death and resurrection and darkness."

Dash had been reading a lot.

He claimed to have read the Bible three times till he knew it backward and forward, and a book called the *Aegyptian Book of Darkness*. He spoke of Kierkegaard and Kant and Buddha and Hesse and Yeats and Eliot and someone named Robert Graves and someone named Colin Wilson and about quantum something, and about transformations and chiaroscuro and shadows.

He loaned books to Mark, and asked him questions about what was in them.

Mark found it all irresistible, although the books were tough to get through.

Only the short stories by Wacey Crossing seemed to be any fun. In them, Crossing wrote about ancient practices that called up creatures of beauty and malevolence. He even mentioned Manosset Sound by name, as if these practices happened there in the 1800s. T.S. Eliot and Robert Graves were a little rougher going, although Mark loved a book called *Demien* by Herman Hesse.

Dash told Mark that, in the dark, everywhere was Nowhere. And it was better to be in the Nowhere than in the Somewhere.

Particularly if you were like one of them.

A bit outcast. A bit funky. A bit eccentric. A bit different.

"Nowhere guys," Dash said.

They loved to say to their parents – when asked, "Where are you going?"

"Nowhere. Honest. Just Nowhere."

And the Nowhere was always dark, and always somewhere else.

BUT MARK DIDN'T EVER GET to meet these "people of the Nowhere," as he began thinking of them.

Dash mentioned them now and again; he acted as if he were getting close to them in some way that wasn't expressed. He became secretive about some of the goings-on when Mark wasn't with him.

"There's a ceremony they have called the Tempting. Each of them cuts his left arm open and spills it over a newly dug grave. They say some ancient words, and begin chanting something I still can't make out. They have these stones and they put the words on them, and dip them in this syrupy mixture, and then put the stones under their tongues, and the words are always inside them after that. Their bodies memorize them or something. They don't even use their minds. It's weird. And then, one of them becomes possessed by the dead person."

Mark assumed it was made-up, stolen from Wacey Crossing's stories, and as a year or so passed, he grew to appreciate Dash's offbeat and dark sense of humor.

Once, together again in some dark place, hanging out, Dash asked, "Do you love me?"

"Excuse you?"

"I don't mean that," Dash said. "I mean, *do you love me.* Like a brother. Like we have a bond?"

Mark thought a minute, feeling uncomfortable with the question.

"Sure. Like a brother."

"We've got to have that bond to make any of it worthwhile. I mean, we'll get married someday and do all kinds of stuff, but if we love each other like that – like brothers – than we can move mountains."

"Sure," Mark said, but decided to turn on the light on the back porch at his parent's house.

He was surprised by what he saw.

Dash sat next to him, but he had a hypodermic needle in his arm, just withdrawing it.

"What the hell is that?"

Dash held the needle up. "It's not for you. Don't worry."

"You a junkie? Dash? What the hell is that?"

"It's not heroin. Jesus, it's the Veil," but Dash would not explain further. He took the needle, covered it, and pressed it into a plastic case that looked more suitable to a toothbrush. "See? I'm not tripping out or anything. Don't freak."

Dash reached up to shut the light off.

Dark again.

Mark sat there wondering if he shouldn't end the friendship or talk to someone at school about what seemed to be Dash's latest self-destructive habit.

But he didn't.

He did what others probably did when their best friends were on drugs – he somehow just put it out of his mind, because Dash never seemed high or wired.

And Mark didn't see much evidence of the hypodermic needle again. Nor did he look for it.

After a few months or so, Mark blocked that moment from his mind. Everything seemed normal, in its own messed up way.

Dash was his only real friend at school, anyway.

ON A NIGHT-SMITTEN COUNTRY ROAD, Dash would flick the headlights off.

Suddenly, it was as if the world vanished. They were in a car with the world gone.

With just a sense of "road." A sense of "nowhere."

Dash started doing the headlight trick before he even had his license. This was back when he had managed to steal his brother's car and sneak out in the night.

He'd pick Mark up down the hill from where he lived. Always after midnight.

Mark would be out there waiting for him, waiting for the adventure.

"I been here forever," he'd say.

"Forever must last about fifteen minutes," Dash said, giving him a gentle punch to the shoulder.

They'd go to parties, or sneak off and grab a burger, or find out where some of the other guys were hanging out, smoking, drinking. Sometimes, they just watched people make out in their cars.

Neither one of them did much wild stuff. Mark even wrote down what he called the Nowhere Manifesto, but he tore it up one afternoon, worried that his mother might find it.

At the end of most evenings, they just called it a night and Dash dropped Mark off at his house.

But, on some nights, Dash took Mark to the graveyard behind the old church.

Mark never saw him draw the needle out again, but he knew that when Dash asked him to wait in the car a second, he might be going into the darkness to shoot up with whatever he used. *The Veil.*

Mark could ignore it. It didn't matter. They were friends.

Mark got out of the car this one time, and

Dash, up near the church, whistled to him to come on up the path to the graves.

IT WAS NOT Mark's church, nor was it Dash's. It was older and more of a historic landmark than a functioning church. All Mark knew about it was that the founding fathers of the area had built it, or built the original building that no longer existed.

The graves behind it had those names like Goody Something and Sir Walter John Something, but most of the gravestones were rubbed smooth and coated with a slimy ooze of moss and yellow-green muck.

A bog, just the other side of a thin line of trees, had flooded the area, so they walked in mud and damp weeds.

"This is where I saw them," Dash said. "This is where they spoke to me. They showed me the Veil for the first time. Here."

Mark glanced around, but they were alone together.

"They asked me to tell them my heart's desire," Dash said. He went over and sat on a long flat stone. He patted the area beside him. Mark went over and joined him. "They told me that the Nowhere needed guys like me. Maybe like you, too."

"Are they some kind of witch cult?" Mark

asked, chin in his hand. He stared across the expanse of field and wood beyond the old church. "Do they worship Satan?"

Dash grinned. "No. Not witches. Not Satan. That's all fairly new stuff. This is older than that. Long before. They're wise people, though. They know things. They believe that they talk to the dead. They believe the dead tell them things. They know the name of all the different gods. The *real* names. The names of power. I don't know how they do. They knew things about me that even my mother wouldn't know. Even you wouldn't know."

"Like what?"

"You don't want to know," Dash said. "There are some things I wouldn't want people to know. But *they* knew."

"Is it about why you had to leave the other school?"

Dash ignored the question. "Want to know something funny?"

Mark shrugged.

"They told me about you. This was before we met. They told me about that thing you did. When you were eleven."

"What thing?"

"You know," Dash said. "With the knife. Don't worry. It's kind of cool."

Dash put his hand on Mark's shoulder. Felt his breath against his ear.

"I did something terrible when I was twelve," Dash whispered. "Something you can't ever tell anyone else in the whole world, or I will hunt you down and kill you and tear out your heart and cut the eyes out of your face. Understood? We're fifteen, but when you're a kid – I mean a little kid – you do things without really knowing why. You're changing. Everything is changing. You have these impulses. You do things because something inside you tells you to do them.

"I once saw the most beautiful dead woman in the world, lying on the ground. She had killed herself, but it left no marks on her because she took pills. She was naked. I was caught doing something to her. But it wasn't what you think. Nothing perverted. She was so beautiful I didn't want to hurt her, even when she was dead and was beyond hurting. And they knew about what I did. They had spoken to her. The Nowhere people. After she died.

"They had gone to where she was buried, and they'd dug her up from the grave. She told them about me, about what I did, and they think I'm some kind of messiah because of it. Like it was a sign that I was the golden child or something."

ON THE PHONE, *the next afternoon, a Saturday:*

"I made it all up. None of it's true," Dash said, and then hung up.

MARK DIDN'T SEE Dash for awhile, but eventually, Mark saw Dash's car idling on the street beneath his bedroom window.

Mark was furious with his father for taking away his stereo because of a drop in grades, and he snuck out the back of the house and got in the car and told Dash, "It's about time you showed your sorry face."

ONCE, they narrowly missed being hit by a car that was following Dash's car too closely. They followed the car for miles just to annoy the driver.

They planned raids on some houses, too.

When a family was out of town, Mark and Dash would go out in the dark, late as they could stand and still feel awake.

They'd break in, way out in some suburban neighborhood. They wouldn't take anything from the home. They'd just get in through some window – it was easy to jimmy one of them open – and see what the house was like on the inside.

They wouldn't disturb anything. They kept the lights out, and wandered room to room.

Dash said he wanted to see how other people lived, what they owned, what they had.

Mark once said it seemed psycho to do it but Dash reassured him that they weren't doing any harm.

Sitting there, on someone else's sofa, Dash

would sometimes speak in some language that wasn't English. They weren't any kind of language Mark had ever heard.

He would say a few of these words and, if Mark asked about them, Dash would say that he hadn't said anything at all.

Sometimes, they'd move a book around on a bookshelf. Or they'd put a CD out of its case and put it on a windowsill. Just enough that it might seem curious to the family, returning from a weekend away.

But this was the worst of what they did together, and it really wasn't much. Some of the other guys at school regularly shoplifted. Others were smoking marijuana half the school day. Others were doing much worse.

Mark assured himself that what he and Dash did was fairly innocent. It really hurt no one. He tried not to think about that needle that Dash had. He didn't really see it, although sometimes he noticed the plastic toothbrush carrier inside Dash's green army jacket.

Although Mark and Dash loved girls and talked about them as much as any other guy in school, they really adored each other. They could've been brothers. Before they'd met – at thirteen – nobody would've thought they resembled each other. But by fifteen, they could've been twins.

Dash made Mark promise to be his Best Man at his wedding, whenever it happened; Mark asked

Dash to be the godfather of his first kid, whenever it came into the world.

In the Nowhere, sometimes, Mark would say things to Dash that he never told anyone else. When Mark got dumped by Emmie, he told Dash first.

When Dash decided he was going to kill himself rather than grow up, he only told Mark.

"That's right," Dash said. "Why turn into some corporate robot and end up like our dads? I'd do it with a knife. I'll become one with the Nowhere. You?"

"Hanging. The front staircase."

"Do it at my folks' place. In the foyer. From the chandelier," Dash said. "In the dark."

They had a good laugh about it, and then shared a cigarette.

"What about those people?"

"What people?"

"The ones," Mark said, grabbing the cigarette from Dash's mouth, "that were in the graveyard. The ones you told me about."

Dash flicked on the light. Regarded Mark with a nearly mistrustful look. His eyes were bloodshot. "Listen, they're dangerous, sometimes. They showed me some things that were kind of nasty."

"Like what?"

Dash shivered slightly. Mark couldn't tell if he was just joking or not.

"Just some really bad shit," he said. "They have these ceremonies that you have to study. I've been studying them for a long time now, and I still don't completely understand them."

"Why haven't I met them?"

"They decide who meets them and who doesn't," Dash said.

"I thought you made them up," Mark laughed again, puffing on the cigarette. "To scare me. You told me you made it all up. Remember?"

"No," Dash said. "I got a little scared. I was worried they might come after you. The priests of the Nowhere are real. They're practically holy. They're really good people, but they do some nasty shit. I'm sort of into what they do."

"Sort of philosophically," Mark added.

"Maybe," Dash said. "Give me that cig back, or go buy a new pack."

DASH WOULD END the night out in the middle of godforsaken nowhere, spinning the car in the mud, or gliding down an icy patch of road, the back-end of the car fish-tailing.

All around them, the dark, as if they drove inside their own minds, and the world existed only for them.

They could talk about their deepest thoughts, argue philosophy, their sense of the meaning of life and if there was one at all. They determined that there was no meaning to life, but to truly enjoy life, they each must act as if there were a meaning to it.

Their understanding of girls became legendary, as they discussed sexual availability versus the sacred virgin as it applied to the girls they knew; misunderstanding of other boys in school, which manifested in an open contempt for jocks and their football parties; they shared their love for Herman Hesse's novels and Joan Armatrading albums and this writer with the unusual name of Wacey Crossing who wrote *When Nowhere Comes* and other books in the 1800s.

Dash owned three Wacey Crossing books, all short stories, and their bindings were leathery and cracked like old Bibles, and inside the books, people had written messy illegible notes all in the margins and drawn what looked like dirty pictures of naked women with huge breasts in the front and back pages.

The Crossing stories were about a mystery cult that had survived centuries of persecution, misshapen creatures that lived beneath graves, and ancient ones that prowled the darkness.

Mark borrowed each of them, and read them thoroughly, enjoying the terribleness of the punishments meted out to those who treated the Nowhere people badly. There were six primary deities in the Crossing stories, all with nicknames: *the Devourer, She Who Befouls The Night, Hallingo-rianang-the-Eater-of-Souls,   Oliara-the-Sword-of-*

Fire, The Swarmgod of the Thousand Stings, The Pope of Pestilence, and *Julaiiar the Conqueror*.

Mark began calling Dash "the Devourer," and he in turn might call Mark "Swarmgod."

It definitely sealed their fates within weirdo-hood. Mark was perfectly happy with that.

They dreamed together, aloud, of what they'd do if they had the powers of Julaiiar the Conqueror who came in Shadow and cut the heads off friend and foe; or if She Who Befouls the Night decided to make it with Oliara-the-Sword-of-Fire, what kind of kid they'd produce.

It all happened when the lights went out.

HEADING DOWN SOME LONESOME ROAD, the headlights off. They'd light their cigarettes, and the world would change from its unsubtle self to some kind of dark wonderland.

Even though Mark might be in the backseat with a current girlfriend making out and doing everything two teens can do with each other while still keeping most of their clothes on, it was Dash who made him feel as if it were just their world: in the car, on a dark road, with nothing but the unexpected wonders of night around.

AND ONE NIGHT, Rachel Cowan had a big party

out at the country place her folks had, a few weeks after graduation, and everybody they knew was going.

Michelle and Danny needed a lift, and even though Dash and Rachel went out once on a date and now didn't get along very well, Mark convinced him to go.

"This is a perfect night for this," Dash said.

"Yeah?" Mark asked, grabbing a cooler of beer. Checked his watch: 10:15. "I figure the party'll be hoppin' by eleven."

"It's a sacred night to the Nowhere. It's a night they call Lifting the Veil."

"Oh," Mark said, used to Dash's tales of the Nowhere and its priests.

Dash whispered to him, as Mark slid into the front seat next to him, "Let's have some fun with them. Okay?"

Mark couldn't reply, because Danny had already gotten in the back of the car, and Michelle rapped at Mark's window for him to unlock her door. In her arms, a plastic and wire cage.

She brought a stupid puppy from her sister's kennels as a surprise birthday gift for Rachel, who had just turned nineteen, and whose dog had recently passed away.

"Just a little fun," Dash said. "For a sacred night."

Then, he reached around to unlock the door for Michelle.

3

THE NIGHT BEGINS

D ash flicked the headlights off.

The night came up like veils of shadow against shadow – purple darkness, black darkness, and the curious ambient light of the earth itself – particles of illumination from unknown sources.

Reflections of slivered moonlight off distant ponds. It was beautiful, Mark thought.

The narrow, winding road was ripe with pot-holes and wounds, and the June-fat trees hung low over it – it was a beautiful world as far as Mark was concerned, and he felt comfortable there with Dash in the front seat, their world, their Nowhere surrounded them.

Mark glanced over at Dash, beside him. Dash in his green army jacket, with holes through out it. Beneath, he wore a black t-shirt. Even in the summer he wore the jacket, his emblem of weirdo-hood, of not abandoning his outcast nature.

Smoke from his mouth. The red glow of the

cigarette lit Dash's features. His hair had gone from brown to dark blue with fiery tinges where it flopped around his eyes. His eyes seemed to have a light of their own.

Dash smiled, showing all his teeth.

It was not pitch black quite yet, for the moon half-lit the world. Its light, diffuse behind scalloped clouds, hinted the outline of a dilapidated farmhouse with its property cut in a ragged square from the encroaching forest, and a balding fringe of dead trees at the edge of the road before the property. A single light glowed in the house, and it somehow made Mark think about loneliness, despite being there with his friends.

He wondered what he would do – now that college loomed, and he and Dash would probably grow out of their friendship, as all friends seemed to after high school. He didn't want it to happen, but there was an inevitability to it – they would move on and stay friends, but lose that closeness, that brotherhood they felt. The farmhouse became a blur as Dash recklessly swung the steering wheel to negotiate a curve in the road.

Then, the woods appeared again, thick and dark, and another turn, another break in the woods cut by a stream and ditch to the left.

They passed what seemed at first an empty, desolate field, and there came the moon across it, a white sickle of moon. It was not empty, but was some kind of cemetery – Mark didn't recognize it at first, but then knew he had been there before –

of course, he thought, it was here, the Old Church is here. Saint Something.

They had been mostly silent in the car – me and Dash in front, our world, our night world.

Mark grabbed another beer from the back, and nearly stuck his hand down Michelle's shirt – she was sure I was making a grab for her, but Danny already had his hand halfway down her shirt, and suddenly something stank like a dead animal in the car, and I knew it was the puppy, in his crate. It was whimpering.

Michelle, after nearly slapping him, reached back and thrust a finger through the small Kari-Kennel opening and murmured, "That's okay, baby, that's okay," then, she reached up and flicked on the car's interior light. "Some light in here would be nice. What's this thing with darkness?"

"Darkness is cool," Mark said.

"Friggin' Goth," Michelle said; Mark was not a Goth. He was just a guy who felt better in the dark. With friends. In the car. It was his comfort zone.

"Are you sure Rachel wants a new dog?" Dash asked. "She can't exactly take it to college with her."

"I already talked to her mom about it. Her mom's going to keep it while Rachel's at Smith."

"She got into Smith?" Mark asked.

"Last minute," Michelle said.

"Where are you two going?" Danny asked, fairly innocently. With the question, came the unspoken: they were a couple to some extent. Mark and Dash were paired in the minds of their classmates.

"How could you not guess?" Michelle huffed. "They've practically been talking about it since sophomore year."

"Oh, yeah," Danny said. "I thought maybe Mark might go to Georgetown."

"I didn't want to go to Georgetown," Mark said. Then, he added, "Really. I didn't."

"U-Mass for us," Dash said.

Mark sniffed at the air. "Who farted?"

"That dog crapped," Dash said. "He needs to go outside. Not in the car."

Mark laughed, popped open the beer, and reached for the radio buttons. Dash rolled down a window, and the humidity poured in – a gentle steam. He switched the air conditioning up to a higher level.

Michelle began lecturing Dash on why the puppy was in the car in the first place, and how Rachel had wanted the puppy ever since her last dog was hit by a car out on the highway; and how, even though we were headed for "what no doubt is going to be some kind of brawl," the puppy would be fine, and when they got to Rachel's house, she'd let it out to do its business in the wild.

"Whoa!" Dash cried out, "that was close!" Another pair of headlights, in the opposite lane from them, fast approaching and crossing the invisible line in the road. Dash swung the car to the right a little too hard, and they all felt the car leaning into the ditch on that side.

Then, back to normal, driving in the dark.

"Do you really want to hurt me?" Mark began singing along with the radio, which he'd very wisely turned up slightly to drown out Michelle's whine. "Jesus, nothing but oldies."

He punched the radio buttons, but the best he could find was a heavy metal.

Briefly, he turned the sound up high; Dash reached over and switched the radio off. Then, he switched it back on, and a voice came up that was nearly monotone, "And the angel carried a crown and a burning sword, and sayeth unto…"

"'Jesus radio. I love it. Selling God on the airwaves without really knowing all about God," Dash said, switching to a soft rock station. "I like oldies better."

"Look," Danny said, rising from the back seat. "I think that's Carbo's truck over there. Hell, did Rachel even invite the dropouts?"

"That redneck," Michelle whispered, as if no one would hear her. "Carbo is such a hillbilly. I'm surprised he ever even got into Gardner." She drew the little yellow puppy from the crate into her arms. She let it lick her all over her face. Her shirt was still unbuttoned, and she wore no bra. Mark could make out the roundish mounds of her breasts, glancing back at her for a second too long.

He found them unappealing. They weren't as big as they looked when covered up.

PERHAPS IT WAS because it was Michelle, whom Mark found generally unappealing.

She had a well-bred look, as if her parents had never been in love, but had know that between their checkbooks, their inheritances, and their basic health, they should mate and produce offspring with equally good checkbooks, inheritances, and health. Like some alien life form that must have progeny in order to conquer the earth.

Michelle was the natural product of this loveless but purposeful union.

He had seen her type throughout high school – she was not a prototype the way Dash was, or even Rachel, who was a true original. She was just one of the herd. Dash had a thing for her, but he said that his interest didn't go much past the flesh.

"She's a copy of a copy of a copy. But with an especially nice rack," he'd said at some point.

Michelle was mass-produced. She was one of many rich girls with not a lot going on other than her birth certificate and her trust fund. She had teeth – and a lot of them – and hair, and a strangely seductive little jaw of determination that waggled side to side when she was pissed off. She dressed like hot stuff, even in her khaki shorts, with visible panty line, and white top wrapped for maximum breastage.

Mark supposed there were boys with the low expectations of a Danny who found her completely irresistible.

But she was no Rachel.

She wasn't even an Emmie, Mark's girlfriend who had dumped him on Prom Night right after they'd made love on the golf course at the Country Club. Right after he'd lost his virginity. Just dumped him, and left him on the moist morning grass as the turgid sun rose somewhere – Mark, there, near the seventh hole, his tux jacket somewhere else in the world, cummerbund lost, shiny black shoes in a sand trap, and carnation shredded from passion.

Still, he had his cufflinks, and a hazy memory of his first time. Emmie had given him that, and she was more of a human being than Michelle could ever hope to be.

Unfortunately, Michelle and Emmie were best friends, so Mark knew that Michelle knew about his getting dumped in that way.

She probably knew about how badly he'd fumbled with Emmie's shiny blue prom dress, how he probably was less-than-perfect at the whole sexual thing and how he may have said something stupid in the throes of *doing-it* that really made Emmie dislike him once and for all.

"You know, that dog has worms," Mark said to her, in the car, still looking at the sloping mounds of her breasts through her open shirt. "And you letting him lick your face could put wet puppy spit full of microscopic worm larvae on your skin, and from there, they could get inside you. And when they do…"

"Only someone like you could come up with something that disgusting," Michelle said.

"I want to hear," Dash said. He drove with one hand; he had a cigarette in the other.

"The puppy has roundworms, and maybe tapeworms," Mark said. "Almost all puppies have them. The puppy will get wormed soon, but right now, that poop inside that little crate probably has tiny strands of spaghetti – that wriggle."

"God!" Michelle shouted, kicking at the back of his seat. "Stop, now. Just stop."

"I want to hear it," Dash said. "So what do they do?"

Mark shrugged. "Well, to dogs and cats, they do a lot. But worming pills will take care of it, most likely. When those worms get into people, it's harder to get rid of them. They make little canals under the skin. They like to go for the eyes."

"You're making that up," Danny said.

"No, for some reason, the roundworms can't mature into adults in people. So the larvae just make do, and they seem to really like getting the tissue around the eyes."

"If," Michelle said, slowly but with her usually dominating force, "you. Do. Not. Shut. Up. Right. Now."

"I won't even go into the tapeworm possibility."

"Jenny Patterson had tapeworm when she was twelve," Dash said. "Remember?"

"No," I said. "I didn't know her back then."

"She had it, and she lost twenty pounds practically overnight. She was sick for a long time. She said it was pretty nasty."

"They grow inside you," Mark said. "They grow as long as they can. They can fill your intestines, and just eat at you."

"I once saw a dead body that was opened up and full of worms," Dash said. "I almost threw up when I saw them in her mouth."

"Shut up!" Michelle shouted.

The puppy began whimpering.

Dash laughed and accidentally dropped his cigarette.

Michelle cried out something that Mark thought was "*What*," and that's when they hit something in the road.

4

THE DEER

The car didn't just hit something in the road.

It slammed into something like a brick wall.

Sounds of brakes squealing, metal crunching and glass breaking filled Mark's ears. He felt the world spin. His head knocked back into the headrest of his seat. He slammed against the glove compartment, almost into the windshield. Something flicked against his scalp.

Michelle screamed. Danny made a noise like he'd had the air knocked out of him. Dash whooped as if he enjoyed the ride; Mark wondered if the puppy was going to be okay.

But it was over in a second.

MARK OPENED his eyes and saw something dark and liquid.

Covering his eyes.

He reached up.

"Shit." He was bleeding. Something had cut his forehead.

Someone touched him on the scalp.

"Not much, Marco." It was Dash. "Just a little blood. It just seems like a lot to you." Then, "Everybody okay back there?"

No answer.

Whatever they'd hit had darted out in front of the car from the edge of the bundle of trees at a bend in the narrow road.

Dash didn't turn the headlights back on. Perhaps they didn't even work. Mark wondered if something awful was going to happen now. If one of them was dead. Or if they'd killed an animal. Or if Dash's parents would ground him and take away all his privileges for the summer and beyond.

Mark wiped his face. It was a lot of blood for a little cut, but he felt the irregular slice at the top of his scalp, and it was, indeed, not much of a wound.

"Lots of bleeding at scalp level," Dash said. He grabbed a tissue and daubed it on Mark's forehead. "See? All better. You knocked it on the dashboard."

"I thought I was dead."

"Maybe you are," Dash said. "Maybe we all are. Maybe we're dead but doomed to stay right here in this wreck and never leave the dark road."

"Hmm," Mark said. "I think I saw that old *Twilight Zone* episode."

From the backseat, Danny gasped, "Oh my god, we hit a deer."

Michelle shouted out "Fuck!"

The word seemed to stretch into an eternity of several seconds.

Outside the car, the world was dark.

For seconds, they were all silent again.

Mark closed his eyes and wished it away. When he opened them again, he was still in the car, feeling bruised, a throbbing at the front of his scalp.

"IS EVERYBODY OKAY?" Dash asked a second time, breaking the quiet. He didn't bother turning around to check. He adjusted the rearview mirror, and glanced back.

"I guess I'm ok," Mark said, although the back of his neck hurt from the way he'd slammed back against the seat. His scalp stung.

"Just a little upside down back here," Danny said. "More beer, please."

"I'm fine. The puppy's fine. As if you care," Michelle said, coughing. "My arm hurts a little. And ow. My knee."

Dash began cussing up a storm. When it subsided, he looked at Mark, tapped him on the shoulder and gave a slight squeeze. "Damn, and I forgot to pay my insurance this month. I am so screwed."

It wasn't a deer.

At least as far as they could tell, although Danny insisted it had antlers, and since he was the drunkest of them, he was the least believed.

MARK GOT OUT LAST, generally pissed off that they wouldn't make it to Rachel's party at all.

They were somewhere between school, and the Sound, and it was a section of road he couldn't quite identify. There were no lights in the distance. There was no traffic noise from some nearby highway. Trees all around, thick with leaves. The moon existed somewhere, but not where Mark stood.

Dash had a flashlight and waved it around the front of the car.

"This car is fucked," Dash said. He spat out some more choice words, and Mark thought it was a bit like watching a three-year-old have a temper tantrum, the way Dash stomped around in a circle, muttering and shaking his head.

"It is, truly," Danny said. He hoisted a beer to his lips, and drank the entire bottle in one gulp. Then, he belched.

The damage to the car was extensive. The front end had completely smashed inward, practically wrapped around the engine; the front axle was bent; and Danny made a joke that it was a miracle none of them was hurt.

"Even the puppy," Danny said. "Man, that was a hell of a deer."

"I didn't see a deer," Michelle said. She had put the puppy on a short leash and walked around the front of the car. "I saw some people. A few of them."

IN THE FLASHLIGHT'S BEAM, she looked like a doll that had been through a windstorm. Pale white, her shirt half unbuttoned, her hair a mess. For a second, Mark thought her lip was cut, but it was just an odd shadow.

"If we hit somebody, they'd be lying here screaming right about now," Danny began, but Michelle gave him a harsh look that shut him up fast.

"I saw these people. I didn't see their faces or anything. I just saw a group of them. Maybe three. Maybe more." She began crying a little.

When the half moon came out from behind a cloud, beyond the trees, casting the slightest amount of light across the road, Mark noticed how her tears shone on her face.

"Somebody hold me," she said.

Danny obliged; his arms wrapped around her. "No, babe, it was a deer. I'm sure it was."

"We killed some people," Michelle said, but

even as she said those words, it didn't sound like she really believed it, seconds after saying it. "They all had shaved heads. They might've been monks or something. I know. It sounds crazy. Maybe it wasn't people."

"We're not far from the old church," Danny said. "Maybe it was some monks."

"I didn't see any monks," Mark said.

"Monks, skinheads," Michelle said with a bit of venom in her voice. "I saw faces. And maybe one of them had antlers on." Then, she laughed. "Oh, my god, it sounds ridiculous. I've had two beers exactly and I sound ridiculous." She looked at Mark and Danny. "You would've seen it if it was people, wouldn't you?"

"Antlers?" Mark grinned.

"What?" Dash let out a huge laugh, like a balloon popping.

"Okay. Something on his head."

"It was dark," Mark said.

"Maybe," Michelle began. Then, seemed to change her thought. "All right. If I saw them, they'd still be around."

"Well," Dash clapped his hands together. "Mystery solved. You got bounced around back there. Maybe it jogged some memory or made you hallucinate."

"Well, I guess you three have talked me out of my mania," Michelle said.

"It was pretty dark, 'chelle, and it happened pretty fast," Dash said. He shook his head, chuckling. "Antler hats. Pretty good. Skinheads in antler hats."

Mark looked at Dash, but couldn't read anything in his face.

IT WAS ONLY LATER, when Dash went to take a leak with Mark, that Dash said, "It was them. The priests of the Nowhere. This is the night."

They stood at the edge of a mossy embankment that encircled what looked like a bog. Thin trees all around. Mark had the uncomfortable feeling that they weren't alone. He kept looking off in the woods as if he would see Danny or Michelle standing there.

Mark toggled his zipper and let loose a stream onto some twigs.

"This is fun, no?" Dash asked. "We're going to be part of a ceremony."

"What are you talking about?" Mark zipped up.

"I guess I didn't tell you. It's a sacred night. Remember in the Wacey Crossing story?"

Mark did. There was a Wacey Crossing story about midsummer's night, and how it was the weakest point of darkness in the world, so the Nowhere gods had their moment to come into the world of Man. It was a bit of a shivery tale, and Mark had a few nightmares after reading it.

"It was just a story," Mark said. "You nut."

"Everything Wacey Crossing wrote was true," Dash said.

Mark nearly looked at Dash straight on, but didn't. It looked like Dash was pulling that toothbrush case-that-didn't-hold-a-toothbrush out of his inside jacket pocket.

Mark didn't want to see the needle come out.

Or see Dash use.

EXCERPT FROM "THE NIGHT OF CHANGING" by Wacey Crossing, from the collection, In The Grave of the Devourer & Others published 1882, N.M. Quint & Sons Press, New York, NY. Used here with permission.

…The one called Rowan motioned to Petra, a flourishing movement of hands that reminded me of fish, swimming. Petra left my side, and I was loathe to let drop her hand, for fear, for the terror I had begun to feel in my heart. She was my beloved, and she was too innocent for this night of madness. Her mind would become twisted from their heathen perversions and dark callings. I looked upon her in the shaded and sickly moonlight, upon her luxurious dark hair, her figure so lovely and dress of gossamer. I was afraid of what this Unholy Man would do to her, what he might take from her, as he had taken my peace from me.

But it was too late. She had persuaded me to bring her, for she longed to speak again to her father. She begged me with tears and cries and silence until finally, weak man that I am, I allowed her to come with me to this ceremony.

Gudrun took her hand, and brought her into the sacred circle, drawing down her cloak, and painting strange figured upon her face and neck.

I did not know what to expect, for although I had been an initiate for nearly a year, I had not borne witness to this highest of their Holy Days, the shortest night of the year at Midsummer. From my studies, I knew that this was the thin sacred veil that flowed between the world of the Nowhere and the world we human beings occupied. The gods were at their most powerless to resist human intervention in their affairs. I was

well aware that invocations would be made, that the Names would be said, and the seven words of power would be intoned over the exhumed grave of one of the early Masters.

The bones of the Masters had been given, relic-like, to the handful of followers left in the world – one some distant European shore, hundreds of thousands of years ago. Each bone, whether a toe-bone or knuckle or entire skull, had been held in secret, and buried with one of the followers, and the circles of belief arose around the grave that held the relic.

I had known that this particular spot of worship held a rib from an early Master. On this rib, these bones, the runes of Boediccaeringon had been carved. These, the last words uttered in a time of famine and torture in the west of the British Isles in those ancient times. It was used, they said, to ward off the invasions of Romans and Norsemen. I had never seen this sacred rib, but now, Gudrun held it.

In the darkness, I saw only its knife-like appearance, curved slightly at the end.

Then, Rowan drew close to her. I saw their shadows nearly touch, and it filled me with both jealousy and dread.

And I knew what he was about. He had lied to me about what this ceremony was – yes, there was truth to his lie. But I knew in that instant that I would forever regret bringing Petra to this blood-thirsty tribe of worshippers.

He was telling her the Words, and the Words were sacred and known only to the few.

And the Words were the names of the Gods, the TRUE NAMES, THE NAMES OF TERRIBLE AND SWIFT POWER, NAMES THAT SHOULD NEVER HAVE BEEN REVEALED TO MANKIND!

To know the secret names of the gods, to be able to say them aloud, had been brought by one who had come back from the dead thousands of years ago. The legend of the Words was that the one who brought them could not get rid of them. They were accursed to the one who knew them, for he could not resist saying them. Could not resist intoning the names of the gods, and this brought terror and panic into the world, and with it, disease and ill-begotten monstrosities. So the first Masters had found a way to put a lock upon them, so that only part of the Names could be said by one, and the Masters knew the completion of the Names – but no Master knew the entire Name to himself alone. The priests that followed the Masters shared the Names as well, and for each gathering, two priests or priestesses would know the Names, and could perform the ceremony if times were needed to invoke the Wrath of Gods. The flesh of the one who heard the Words could not resist saying them, for the Words went worm-like not into the brain, but into the lips and the throat, and remained there until the point of Death.

Only in the last throes of Death would the Words emerge.

I knew then to what end they used my beloved Petra.

God have mercy on my soul that I had ever taken the woman I loved into their corrupt circle! Petra had been living within a world of despair since her dear father had died so horribly! Had I but known the lengths she would go to in order to reach him, in order to be with him again!

She herself took the sharpened bone and thrust it into her breast, and as she died, I heard her utter some insane language, a string of vowels and consonants that made no earthly sense. She fell; the others held me back, though I fought them dearly to get to her.

Rowan crouched down, a lion over its kill, and leaned into her ear to whisper something.

I struggled free and escaped my captors. I fled deep into miasmic bogs and woods, running from the terror and evil of it all. The visions of what I'd seen in the dark, of the dancing and singing of the priests and their minions, their shadows against the darker shadows of night, and within their circle, Petra, dying – and with her last breath, the demonic language!

At my apartment on Broad Street, I locked the door, and shuttered the window from the night. I lit candle after candle and lamp after lamp, to bring the brilliance of day into the late hours.

I heard a rapping at my door at nearly three in the morning.

She had found me. She had returned to me.

How could I resist her? She was my heart. She was my soul.

For her, I snuffed the candles, and turned down the lamps.

I left the Nowhere into my room. My soul.

Petra found me, before the morning had come.

She showed me the visage of a god whose true name should have been destroyed millennia ago. In the ancient tongue of the Chaldeans and Babylonians, a savage, devouring god whose hunger for children and the innocent is never-ending....

5

SHELTER

Mark and his friends found nothing in the ditch on the side of the road. Neither were there any people – or deer – moaning in the woods.

"Whatever it was, it was big and strong."

"Brilliant deduction," Michelle said.

"A bear, maybe," Dash said.

"We got bears out here?" Danny asked.

Michelle flipped out her cell phone. The green light came up, and she began punching in numbers. "You have triple A, Dash?"

"No."

"Who you callin'?" Mark asked.

Michelle turned her back to them.

Then, she said, "Rachel? It's 'chelle. Listen, Dash wrecked his car out – no, we're okay. Oh my god, I know," she said, her voice dropping to a whisper as she said stuff that Mark was sure had to do with what geeks they were and how she'd been stuck riding with them because Danny was too drunk to drive. Then, her voice returned to normal. "No, no idea. We're not far from some farmhouse. And a graveyard. Yep. We have a special gift for you. I am not telling. Can you send your brother out to Route --Rachel? Rachel? You're breaking up. Damn it," Michelle said, slapping her phone shut. She spun around. "You guys have a cell phone?"

"I'm technologically challenged at the moment," Dash shrugged, and went to grab a beer from the back of the car. When he got there, scrambling around the backseat, he shouted, "Jesus, Danny, did you drink two six packs?"

"I don't think so," Danny said, looking at both Michelle and Mark with the look of an innocent puppy. "Did I?"

"Found one. Wait, found three. No, five. Who wants a beer?"

"I do!" Mark shouted.

"Yeah," Danny said.

Michelle opened her cell phone again, and tried dialing. "We're in one of those dead areas."

"Dead?" Danny grinned.

"Can't get through," Michelle said, practically under her breath. She went over and stood beside Mark, and touched him lightly on the shoulder. "I guess we can't just walk to the party? Jesus, Danny, you always have that damn cell phone."

"We can find another phone," Dash said. "There's that church."

"Or the farmhouse."

"Church is closer. There's either going to be a payphone or an office phone in there."

The sky began dripping with rain. The soft distant rumble of thunder.

"It's coming back," Danny said. "One-one-thousand, two-one-thousand."

A few seconds later a flash of lightning hit that was so bright it seemed to illuminate the forest, and for a moment, Mark thought he saw people standing there, behind some trees.

Danny began counting again, and a louder rumble of thunder sounded.

The rain began coming down fast, and Dash called out, "Come on, this way," and Michelle put the puppy in the little carrier; Danny took it in his left hand and held her hand with his right, and they ran together. Mark jogged behind them all, down the now-slick road.

Within minutes, Dash ran to the right, up the grass-covered path that led to the Old Church. Mud sloshed all around. The rain came down in sheets, and Danny was laughing and running, and the puppy in the carrier was barking; Mark held the flashlight up so they could see their way up the path, and couldn't wait to get inside the church and be dry again.

As they got closer to it, Mark noticed that there was a flickering light from within the church.

"GOD, we should've just stayed in the car," Michelle said.

She was soaked, her hair, dripping, her shirt pasted to her breasts. "This feels a little déjà vu in the junior high department. I can't wait to get out of this place and get to Northampton. May this be my last rainy night in Manossett."

"Yeah," Danny said. Then, he added, "God, I feel wasted."

"I'm amazed you're on your feet," Michelle said, nearly cheerfully.

"I can always go down the road to that farmhouse, too," Mark said, not breaking eye contact with Michelle.

"No need, Marco," Dash said.

They huddled inside the arched doorway of the church, Mark pressed against the thick wooden door.

"This is more of a chapel than an actual church," Dash said. "It's one of the oldest in this area."

"It's locked," Danny said.

THE WINDOWS WERE all shuttered and locked from the inside, as well – Mark had checked when they'd first arrived.

Lightning lit the night again, and Mark saw

the rocky graveyard lit up. Again, he thought he saw people – a group of them there – but they seemed blurred to him, and he wasn't sure if perhaps he should quit drinking beer.

"This kind of place," Dash said, "has to have a key. This isn't the kind of hangout people worry about getting broken into. Not way the hell out here."

He felt around in the recesses of the arch as it peaked and then dipped, and cried out, "Gotcha!"

He held up a thin round key. "Ask and it shall be given to you."

"Thank god," Michelle said. "I just want to be somewhere dry."

Mark kept looking out through the heavy rain at the darkness of the graveyard. He heard the door open behind him. The puppy whimpered in its carrier, and Danny made baby noises to it as he lifted it and took it inside.

One-one-thousand, two-one-thousand.

The sky lit up with whiteness.

There, in the graveyard, shadows of people.

And what looked like an open grave.

Then, darkness. Rain. The grumble and crack of thunder.

"THE WORLD'S SMALLEST CHAPEL," Dash said. "You probably know its history."

The chapel was one oblong room, with angles

cut into it to create recesses with shrines along its gray stone walls.

Mark noticed the windows first – barely slits to let in light, with stained glass in them. The shutters outside were deceptive – they were large, and made Mark think the place had large windows as well. When he and Dash had been in the grave-yard before, they'd never thought to venture in the church itself. It was a plain, nearly bare church, with flat, long benches for pews. The altar looked very much like a wide flat stone of four or five feet in length, and two feet wide.

There were fat long candles in brass holders up and down the aisles, all lit.

"Well, there's no phone here," Michelle said. "At least it's dry."

"Yeah. And it's better than being out there."

"How's the puppy?" she asked.

Danny crouched beside the carrier and looked in. "Doing fine. Chewing on his rawhide."

"Damn," Dash said. "My ciggies are ruined." He held his pack of Marlboros up.

"I have some," Mark said. He reached into his pocket, and drew out two cigarettes. "Got a lighter?"

"I do," Danny said, feeling in his pockets.

"I got matches," Dash said, withdrawing some from within his jacket. "And shockingly, they're dry. Five left." He struck one against the match-book, and Mark passed him a cigarette.

"You keep these," he passed the matches to

Mark once he'd begun puffing on the cigarette. Mark thrust the matches into the back pocket of his jeans. "You got four more cigarettes and four more matches. Perfect, Marco."

"I hope Rachel appreciates the effort we go to for her birthday," Michelle said. She reached into her handbag and withdrew a comb. She ran it through her hair, her head tilting sideway. She wandered over to one of the pews near the front of the chapel. "So now what?" She patted the bench where she sat, and Danny sat down beside her. Soon his arm was around her waist, and she leaned against his shoulder, looking up at the candles at the altar. "This is one ugly chapel. Those puritans really – holy crap, look at that!" she pointed toward the curved wall behind the altar.

Mark immediately looked up. Behind the flickering candle, there was a painting that reminded him of something from his sophomore European History book. It was nearly medieval looking – a faded painting of what seemed to be several monks, their heads shaved in tonsure.

"Those look like the guys I saw," Michelle gasped, and then giggled. "How bizarre."

"Oh yeah, the monks we hit," Dash said, his voice brimming with contempt. "The ones wearing antlers."

"Gives me the creeps, a little," Michelle said. "Now I really wish we'd stayed in the car."

"And risk getting hit from behind by another car? No thank you," Dash said. "What good would that do? Your cell phone won't work. I know this place. I'm sure there's a phone in it."

Mark said something about how seeing a painting of monks in a chapel was not the strangest thing in the world, but the whole time he felt like he was lying. Wasn't sure why, but there was something funny about the painting.

He walked up the aisle to get a closer look. Stepped up the worn, uneven stone steps to the altar.

The monks had faces that were like softened inverted triangles, and large wise eyes. There were four of them. In one of their hands, there was what looked like a thin white flute that bore mark-ings – *Hebrew? Latin?* Mark had no idea. As he gazed at it in the shimmering candlelight, he thought it might be the thin tusk of some wild animal rather than a flute. One of the monks held a round stone in his hand, or perhaps it was a large wafer of some kind. Again, this had strange marking upon it. The third monk held both his hands out. The third monk's hands were merely presented as having nothing in them.

But the fourth monk in the group held a small human skull in his hands.

The skull had small bumps along its scalp – two just above the forehead. And its front row of teeth seemed unusually sharp, nearly wolf-like.

"IT's FUNNY," Mark said.

Behind him, Michelle. She had gotten up and looked around the altar, too. "What?"

"I was sure I'd been in here once. A long time ago. Some time. But I guess I never have. I've been outside before. But never in here. I've never even seen anyone go in here before."

"Look at this," Michelle said. He turned, and she was reading something off the top of the slab.

He went to look. The stone tablet was covered with a stubble of mold or some kind of dusty lichen. Michelle brushed some of it off. "Look at that, Mark," she said, pointing to something carved into the stone.

Mark thought the drawing was a squiggle of circles and lines intersecting – some abstract Christian imagery. He noticed that it had eyes.

"It's some kind of bird," she said.

"Or bug. Look at its wings. There are four of them," Mark said. In his mind, the words *Swarmgod of the Thousand Stingers* seemed to surface. Words beneath the carved figure. "Is this Aramaic or something?"

"It's Latin," Dash said from the back of the room. "Or Greek."

"I took Latin in ninth grade," Michelle said. "It doesn't look like anything I remember."

"Then it's Greek," Dash said. "I've been in here before. I got a guided tour. This is one of the oldest churches in New England."

"How old?" Michelle asked, idly, her eyes never leaving the altar top.

"I would guess the 1600s."

"No, wait, I know what language this is. This is just French," Michelle said. "It's just carved in the stone with such a strange script, I didn't notice it. Let's see, this means, no, maybe it's not French. It's something I recognize." She leaned against the stone tablet. "Why would the pilgrims write in Greek? Or French?"

"I'm sure more than just pilgrims have been using this in the past five hundred or so years," Mark volunteered.

"That's right," Dash said.

"This is Latin, this part of it." Michelle's fingers traced the engraving. "VE. DEU. VI. Well, it's all broken up. It could mean anything. And what the hell is that? It looks like a round mouth full of sharp teeth."

"Deu is probably Deus," Mark said. The words seemed to be in his head: *The Devourer. She Who Befouls The Night. The Pope of Pestilence.*

"Maybe," Michelle nodded. "These drawings are fascinating. They almost look like caveman paintings. This word – AMOR. That's easy. Unless it's part of a longer word – too bad it got rubbed away here. I just wish I could figure out the letters in between."

"I didn't know you studied Latin," Mark said.

"Two years, but I switched to French junior year. I stopped enjoying it," Michelle said. Then she arched an eyebrow. "What, you think I'm just some dumb rich girl skating through life?"

"No, no, really, I don't," Mark said.

"Well, there's always more to people than you think. Even you and your buddy," Michelle offered a sweet smile. "I'll probably major in comparative lit at Smith, if I can take German and handle it at the same time. Someday, maybe I'll translate great works of literature. Or be a foreign correspondent."

"Or a spy," Dash said.

Mark almost wanted to tell Dash to shut up. He had his own interest in language, and had been studying Spanish in school, but had wanted to learn French, too. He looked at Michelle carefully, as if seeing her for the first time. She noticed, and laughed.

"I guess it takes a car wreck and a storm for us to get along," she said. He felt warmth from her, just standing beside her. Connecting in some way that he never thought he could with a girl like Michelle.

"Well, obviously, there's no phone here," Dash said. "Maybe we better take a hike."

"Yeah," Mark said, feeling a bit more like a man.

"I'll be fine here. I'm going to try and decipher this stuff," Michelle said. "Danny, you want to go with them?"

Danny, the puppy in his lap, made a motion

that seemed to indicate that the puppy needed him.

"Me and Mark will go to that farmhouse," Dash said. "You two stay here. What, it's maybe a mile down the road?"

Mark nodded. "Yeah."

"We can run."

"Sure," Mark said, but dreaded the rain.

"You two just continue the party here, dry off, and we'll be back," Dash said. "Feel free to chug the last beer, Danny."

THE RAIN HAD SLOWED to a steady but light sprinkling. The lightning was off in a distant sky, barely lighting the path from the old church.

"Okay, now, here's what we do," Dash said.

"What's all this?" Mark said.

"Huh?"

"'Huh?' You planned this," Mark said. "I know you did. What *is* all this? The church. The crash. Huh?"

"Come on, Marco, I told you, we'll have a little fun."

"It's not fun. It's the opposite of fun. Fun would be the party. Fun would be anywhere but here."

They walked out among the graves. Mark kept the flashlight on the ground to avoid any rocks and stones.

"She's a bitch, you know that? Don't let her fool you with all that Latin shit. She spent half of high school thinking that guys like you and me are less than toads, so don't suddenly get all sugary just because she shows you her rack."

"Maybe we *are* less than toads, Dash. Maybe all this Nowhere crap makes us warts on toads."

"Blasphemy." Dash reached over and slapped him hard on the face.

It stung. Mark reached up and touched his cheek.

"Tonight is the night." Dash said grabbed him by the elbow, and pulled him close to him. The flashlight fell from Mark's hand. Dash's breath was all beer. "Look, you've known since you were thirteen that you were going to be part of this. You knew. And tonight is the night. Just like in the book. It's the Night of Lifting the Veil. It is nearly midnight. It is midsummer's night. The shortest night of the year. The night when the Veil between our world and the world of the Nowhere is thinnest."

Mark laughed. "Come on, Dash. Come *on*."

He pulled away from Dash, walking ahead on a narrow, scraggly path between gravestones. "Get real."

Then, Mark thought he saw something before him – some shape that was all shadow, and he saw that at the edge of the graveyard, like a gate, there were people standing there, in long coats or cloaks, he wasn't sure, but he could see them.

He heard Dash groan behind him.

Sound of sudden movement.

Mark was about to turn around to see what was wrong, when something hit him hard on the side of the head, and he was out.

MARK AWOKE A FEW SECONDS LATER, feeling dizzy. His vision blurred. All shadows and scant moonlight around him.

The rain kept coming down.

He lay in mud.

He thought he saw others there, those people, those monks, whoever and whatever they were, and it seemed nearly natural to see them. He almost expected them. Had it all been true? Had everything Dash had been telling him about the Nowhere – all those stories – been true?

He lay there, blinking, in the rain.

Of course, a cult could survive. There were all kinds of cults and religions in the world. But right here? In Manosset, in the 21st century? And could they be so backward and ignorant as to truly believe that there were gods with such ridiculous names as She Who Befouls the Night?

But those were just nicknames. He knew that from the Wacey Crossing stories. All names for the gods were not their true names. Their true names were only known by those who held the power.

The back of his head throbbed.

He looked up into Dash's face, shadowed with night.

Were they alone? He felt alone.

"Here's the thing. You've got to listen very carefully, Marco. Very carefully. There are words, and they're on this," Dash pressed something into Mark's hand. His fingers curled around it instinctively. "Sometimes, the god that enters gets out of hand. And has to be stopped. The words will stop the god. The words are the only thing that stops the god. Listen. Just lie there and listen or I will hit you again so hard so help me god Marco you might never wake up. Listen! This is so important," Dash said.

Was he weeping? Was it rain? Mark couldn't tell.

"I have to fulfill something here. It is my destiny. I am chosen for something, and tonight is the night. When this happens – and it has only happened nine times since the dawn of recorded history, Marco, nine times, I will be the tenth. I will be the tenth, and this hasn't been arrived at lightly. They are very smart people. They have waited more than a thousand years in their religion to allow this to happen again. They feel it's time. And I am the one. But you have got to remember the words when you hear them, Marco. I can only say them once. You are the only one who can stop this with the words. Only the one I...I," Dash's voice broke.

Then, strength returned.

"Only the one I have given my heart to can stop this once it starts. And the words have got to be remembered. These others," Dash nodded to darkness, although Mark saw no one, "they have had their tongues cut out lest they utter the words. The one who told me, taught me, drilled me in this -- he's dead. I can say the words to you, but you must remember them. And with the words, I will tell you the names of the gods. This is an enormous responsibility. The world is corrupt. The time of human life is nearly over. The gods want to return and end the stupidity of this race of men. The names of the gods," he leaned into Mark's face, and pressed his mouth to Mark's ear, he began whispering something that Mark tried to remember as soon as he heard it.

"There's really a Nowhere?" Mark asked, pleading in his voice.

"Oh," Dash sighed. "Marco, wait til to you see it. I mean really see it. There's something you need to drink. Here, sit up."

Mark felt Dash's hand slip behind his neck. "It's easier to see like this."

Mark moaned a little – the pain at the back of his scalp intensified. "You hit me too hard."

"Sorry." Dash withdrew the hypodermic needle from the plastic case.

"What – what are you – what – don't," Mark whispered.

"It'll take the pain away. And you'll under-stand. You'll see. You will really see," Dash said, and he held Mark's arm down, tore his shirtsleeve up to his bicep. Dash squeezed his bicep, and then Mark felt the needle go in, twisting into his flesh.

"This isn't junk. This is ambrosia. Believe me," Dash whispered. "You'll have a taste of the Nowhere. What it really can be like."

THE SENSATION OF FLOATING, but not floating.

Hands moved in bird-like blurs before his eyes.

It was already morning. The rain had stopped. The sun was out.

But the sun was white, not a warm yellowish gold, it was white – all the light was pure white in the sky.

Mark sat up against the gravestone. The throbbing in his head was gone. The trees were funny, the woods seemed weird. Something moved along the bark of the trees. Snakes and worms wriggled along them.

The strange thing was: some things were missing. The trees themselves didn't move in a light wind; and there was no rain, although there had been second before.

Dash was there, only he was Dash with a difference: he seemed better looking. Color in his face. A rosy glow. His eyes were like a little boy's – all happy and expectant. Mark's eyes went in and out of focus. He heard a strange humming in his head. He looked at his hands, and he saw them as liquid, contained within some invisible boundary that defined "hand." When he waved his hand, some molecules of flesh dispersed – just a few -- and seemed to form into an insect of some type in the air – a ladybug, flying off.

"Ain't it cool?" Dash asked. "It's like the world only different. If you stay still, you disappear. Watch."

Dash closed his eyes and mouth, and clasped his hands together. Within seconds, he seemed to evaporate like steam.

Then, he laughed, and suddenly was there again. "The world we're used to has to move a lot or make noise for things in the Veil to see it. Otherwise you become invisible, even to the gods. It's a strange place, no?"

Dash kept laughing, but it all seemed to move slowly, and Dash drew back his black t-shirt, tearing it, only it didn't tear like fabric. It formed droplets of black goo that absorbed against his green jacket.

Then, Dash pressed his hand against his pale, hairless chest and drew back the skin – not as if it were cut or scraped, but in that liquid medium, as if Dash himself were a soap bubble – malleable and shifting, but within a boundary that kept the liquid in place.

Dash's fingers went deeper into his flesh. He drew out what appeared to be a pulsing mass of purple and poppy red.

Smiling, Dash brought it closer to Mark's face.

"My heart," he said. "My heart and your heart."

Dash reached into Mark's chest, and it tickled. Mark laughed, and felt Dash's fingers inside his flesh, moving along the organs within his ribcage.

A feather-like tickle of his heart.

All the while, the liquid between their bodies, the floating droplets, merged and mixed, splashing together.

Dash held both hearts for Mark to see.

"We're brothers," Dash said.

"The Veil," Mark murmured, feeling particularly good, as if he had never know what it meant in life to feel good.

Dash nodded. "Yep. The Veil. From a garden that existed thousands and thousands of years ago. A garden destroyed by mankind when it learned the secret names of the gods. But the wise ones who knew its value rescued this flower and its seed. And they've planted it and cared for it in secret all these years, Marco. And it shows you the real world. The Nowhere. If I told you this was Eden itself, wouldn't you believe me? Look, we flow. Look at the sky. This is night, Marco. Not daylight. This is true night. The blackness is an illusion. See? Look –" Dash pointed to the sky. An eel wriggled in the white air as if it were moving through rippling milk. "This is the realm of the gods. This is what we're blinded to. This is what the Nowhere people know. And always have. We can't be here long. We can't take the Veil too much. It's addictive, but it can be horrible as well as beautiful. Do you see now? Marco? How beautiful? Marco, I've seen magnificent cities on the surface of the sea – I've seen creatures that have only been drawn in ancient texts – sea monsters, mermaids, all here, all within the Veil. And the gods, too. They cause what happen in our world, but we are blinded and cannot see – we see through darkness. The Nowhere is the true light."

"I feel a little sick," Mark said, reaching to his stomach. "Sick."

"It's your first time. But you'll get used to it. You'll enjoy it more. Right now, you can only tolerate a few minutes. But later, you'll be able to have more of it. I'll show you amazing things, brother. Amazing. One more beautiful than the next," Dash said, and then he held something in the air. It looked like a white horn -- *or an animal bone?* Writhing around it, tiny red insects. "You'll come out of this in a minute or two, Marco. When you do, you must say the names as soon as I've said the first part. And if it gets too much out of hand, you can stop it. There's always a way to stop it. Just remember the Words. They're here, on this bone. See?" He said them quietly and made Mark repeat them. "The Words are hard to remember. But once you hear the names you can't forget, even if you try. You hear them and your molecules take them in and hold them. The flesh remembers. You have to say the names as soon as you see me die."

"Die?" Mark looked at him, uncomprehending. "You're going to die?"

"Not really. Not die like you think. You ready?" Dash held the bone in front of his chest.

He began saying the first halves of the names of the gods of the Nowhere.

ALONE, with Dash, in the rain.

Out of the Veil. In the real world. The ordinary, awful world again.

Mark sat up.

Sky, black. The earth, sucking mud.

Taking the smooth thin bone, Dash pressed the sharpened end of it into his chest.

Mark reached for the bone, pulling it out. "No, Dash, please, no!"

As he let out a final breath, Dash whispered the names of the gods.

WHEN DASH'S eyes were closed, Mark said the last half of the names. He didn't know how he could remember them – they were a long string of sounds and clicks and howls. They hurt his ears to say, like a strangely out of tune sound of pipes being played from his throat.

He almost wanted to say the Words, as well, out of fear.

The Words that could stop this.

But he hesitated. He tried to think of the Words, but none of them came to him. He tried to remember Dash's voice speaking them, but it was like a wall of silence.

Dash opened his eyes again.

They glowed like the ends of cigarettes in the dark.

6

THE CHURCH

Mark began shivering in the darkness as he watched what had been Dash rise to its feet. It no longer seemed to be Dash, not in the sense that he had felt Dash had been. It had glowing eyes, and its teeth were sharp at the ends, small nails of teeth, and even in the moonlight, Mark could see the way spurs had burst from his joints -- elbows and knees -- and writhing worms, long night-crawlers, moved along his fingers.

"Nowhere is here," Dash grinned, and for a second, Mark thought it was a trick.

The drug, perhaps. Still lingering in his system.

Of course. The drug. The Veil.

The needle that had gone in his arm.

"Jesus," Dash said. "I'm *hungry*."

DASH TURNED, glancing toward the church. Then, back to Mark. "You're not going to understand this, Mark. If you could see what I see, you would."

The red eyes burned and then seemed to fade into Dash's normal eyes.

Mark heaved a sigh – it must've been the drug. He was still hallucinating. He still felt weak and dizzy, and he had to sit down again. His head was spinning.

It was the drug. That's all it was. None of it had happened.

"Look, give me a minute," Dash said. "You need to rest. You're going through a lot. Shit, I've been through a lot."

Mark turned, and threw up onto a gravestone. He wiped his mouth; a sickly sweet taste lingered in his throat. *The Veil.*

When he turned around, Dash was gone; by the time Mark rose up on his feet, he thought he saw some enormous winged bird – almost a pterodactyl, given its wingspan – landing at the door to the old church; but it was a man – no, it was Dash.

Mark walked toward the church, lurching with each step, stopping every few feet to cough.

God, what if I die? What if that drug kills me? He slid in the mud and had to pick himself up. His heart beat rapidly. It was poison. I'm going to die.

By the time he reached the door to the old church, he heard Danny's shout.

THE CANDLES along the altar were lit. It was warm and humid within the church, as if the summer storm had turned it into a steam room.

"What the fuck?" Danny laughed. "Holy shit, what the hell have you been drinkin', Dashy? Or maybe it's me, maybe it's just me!" He was beer-soaked at this point; the last couple of bottles of beer lay beside him on the stone altar. Michelle glanced up – they were making out, which is what they seemed to do whenever they had five minutes to themselves.

"Dash, don't, just – just – get away," Mark shouted from the doorway. He stepped into the back of the church. "Just come outside!"

"Oh Danny boy, the pipes, the pipes are call-in'," Dash began to sing, and practically skipped into the church. Danny had his pants off, briefs intact, button-down shirt still on with a few buttons missing; Michelle's shirt was open; she made an annoyed sound in the back of her throat.

"Sorry to interrupt, lovebirds," Dash said.

"Get the hell outta here," Danny said, but he began laughing – it must have struck him as funny to be caught nearly doing it with his girl on the altar of this rat-hole church.

Michelle pushed Danny away and began closing her shirt up.

"Enough," she said.

"Just a little fun," Dash said.

Mark stood at the entrance to the church, watching Dash, unsure of what he was really seeing. Dash seemed to move with a grace he'd never had before, like a dancer or gymnast, and he went right up to the altar and pressed his hands down on two of the candles to snuff them out.

Only one left.

"Dash!" Mark called out. "Come on, let's go. This won't be fun."

Dash turned back to him, and in the final candle's glow, laughed a little – laughed the way he would when they'd first met, back in eighth grade, a *let's-have-fun* laugh, and said, "Oh, wait and see."

Then, he snuffed the last candle out. The room was plunged into darkness.

"Hey, who turned off the lights?" Danny shouted.

Mark saw shadows against shadows. Michelle started cussing, and saying she just wanted to get the puppy and get to the party, and why didn't her cell phone work? Danny began laughing and telling her that it was going to be better in the dark, but Mark heard a strange groaning sound.

The door behind him slammed shut, as if by a great wind.

But there had been no wind.

And then, the screaming began.

MARK'S first instinct was to run away; but he

moved forward in the darkness, hitting against one of the long benches. He dug into his jeans for the matches, and drew them out.

Only four left in the matchbook.

He lit one, and for a fizzing few seconds, the light lit up the room – there was Michelle, screaming, and something with enormous leathery wings, and crab-like appendages studding its body – it was Dash but it was no longer Dash –it had hold of Danny by the throat and was shaking him hard, side to side.

The match went out.

ANOTHER MATCH; he struck it, and it flared up for a moment.

Michelle was running toward him, halfway there– her eyes were wide and seemed to have lost all intelligence –

A creature that seemed both insect and dragon – it was only an impression, like the flash of a dream – chewing on Danny's scalp --

Mark dropped the match. Darkness blinded him.

GURGLING SOUNDS FOLLOWED, and then the wet shredding noise and cracking of bones.

He heard footsteps near him -- *Michelle?* Brushing past.

Dash's voice:

"Ye*sssss*," snakelike and hollow. "Marco, the Nowhere is here, you helped bring it, it's all true," and then the sounds of a dreadful slobbering and gobbling, as of a wild dog swiftly devouring prey.

MARK DREW OUT A THIRD MATCH, and struck it in the matchbook.

Dash stood so close to him that they were practically touching.

Shocked by the closeness, Mark dropped the match, and it went out.

IN THAT SECOND, he had seen the white and pink worms encircling Dash's throat and hands, growing in pulsating movements from his flesh, and soft fuzzy tendrils gently fluttering from his bare waist and ribcage.

His mouth painted a dark red.

In his arms, he cradled what was left of Danny's body. Torn and ragged, more meat that human.

"Any shape I desire," Dash said, and tossed Danny's remains to Mark when the darkness again engulfed him.

MARK FELT nausea sweep through him. He dropped the body and turned to run, but fell to his knees instead.

"Pray to your little god," Dash said. "Pray like a good altar boy. But you're in the wrong place, Marco. This is the altar of the Nowhere. The Church of the Veil. Now, where do you think Michelle's run off to? Not outside. I made sure the door was shut tight and locked. She must be here. Hiding. Oh, yeah! This makes it more of a game, doesn't it? But I can see with more than eyes now. You know that, Marco. You've been through the Veil. You know that it's a world of liquid white now."

Mark wanted to cry out, or scream, but his voice had abandoned him – or else he had screamed so much in the past few moments – without realizing it -- that he had none left. He felt cold and hot at the same time.

The Words. Remember the Words.

You can stop him with them. They're the words of ending. The god will return to the Veil. The Words. He imagined the bone with all the scratching on it. Dash's voice saying the Words and making him repeat them back.

Some kind of trick.

"I can hear her breathing," Dash said. "She's gonna love what I do to her. I hope you're there to see it, Marco. I hope you'll partake."

Mark thought he heard Michelle cry out from behind him.

"Run! Get out! Michelle! Just get out!"

The sound of her sobs echoed.

"It's locked!" she cried out, banging on the door, "Somebody! Somebody help me! Help!"

"Michelle! Shut up! Just shut up!" Mark yells. "Stay still and shut up!"

It needs movement and noise. Maybe it will leave now that it had Danny. Dear Jesus help us. Help her.

The Words.

Remember them.

7

IN DARKNESS, THE ENDING

*A*nd so, in the room in the church, the thing in the dark feels his ankles.

He presses himself against the wall, halfway between scared shitless and ready to do something – *anything* – to keep it from going after Michelle.

Slick and sticky and wormy, it seems to lick his calves with its feelers.

Michelle by the door, moaning out little noises.

The thing that Dash has become slithers and feels its way over to her.

In Dash's mind, he must be seeing the whiteness of the darkness. He must be seeing the liquid move and the unseen things that wriggle in the air and along the walls.

Dash must see Michelle, too, not as a terrified young woman of eighteen, but as some collection of molecules to be devoured, to be fed upon, to increase its happiness and its mission as it moves through the world, but sees and feels all through the Veil that Dash has now destroyed within himself.

The last of the tendrils that Dash-thing drags with him slides away from Mark's foot.

Leaving him. Letting him go.

Moving toward *her*.

She is groaning as if she can't contain her fear.

And then, she lets out a bloodcurdling scream – and another, and another in quick succession.

HE HEARS THE THROATY LAUGH.

"Come on, it's only me, Michelle, come on," Dash says, and for a fleeting instant Mark thinks that it might be a game. It might just be all fake. *The drug. Yeah, it's the drug. It was some kind of illusion. Some trick of light and dark. A bad acid flashback.*

This is some kind of trip. This isn't the real world.

Michelle's sobbing, with diminishing screams in her voice, jagged shards of sound.

Get to Danny. Something on him. His jacket. Jeans.

A lighter.

It's afraid of light. The Nowhere can't exist where there's any light.

Any genuine light.

If darkness is light to it, then surely light is its own kind of darkness.

"You always wanted me, Michelle, you always did," the thing that Dash has become says. "Rachel told me how you thought I was quirky and cool. When she did, when she whispered those things to me, it got me so revved up, baby. I knew that someday you and I would have this moment."

Mark hears the whirring sound again – a soft, rapid fluttering.

If I just get to Danny's jacket, Mark thinks. *The lighter.*

"Please," Michelle whimpers. "Dash, please. Don't hurt me. Please. Oh god. Please."

Her "please" becomes bleating like a sheep. In a horrible way it's funny, it sounds like a joke, but Mark knows it's not.

Why doesn't she try to run? Is it blocking her way?

Mark estimates that he can get to the doorway.

To where Danny's body rests.

Just grab the jacket and thrust his hand into the pockets.

He can get the lighter, flick it up, and scare the monster away.

"Oh, Michelle, baby," it says. "I want to love you so badly. I want you to be my girl, don't you know that?"

"Please," she says in such an awful tone that tears came to Mark's eyes even as he takes a step toward the opposite corner of the room.

"Take my hand, Michelle, don't be afraid," it says. "I want to love all of you in every way."

The sound changes – it feels like an alarm has gone off somewhere. A sound like hissing and spitting and the crack of a whip.

"No!" Michelle screams, "Oh my god, oh my god, god, god, god, god." Her screams turn into giggles and jets of laughter.

Mark races to Danny's body, pushing through the wetness, tearing the shorts from what remains of the lower half of him, sifting quickly through the pockets until he finds something cylindrical and hard.

The lighter.

Hang on, Michelle.

The sounds are wet and bubbling.

Mark turns, flicking the lighter.

Doesn't light up.

Flick!

Again no light.

Then, a spark.

A SMALL FLAME erupts from the lighter.

He cups it in his hand, a yellow and rosy glow around his palm.

He calls out to Dash, but the splattering noise and that whirring has begun again.

Mark brings the flame up to see:

Shadows cast against the old bare wall of the room.

He sees what looks like the spread wings of a gigantic shiny beetle. Long white and pink worms –slender tentacles – move between Dash's body, which floats barely a foot in the air – holding Michelle – caressing her – she struggles against it -- the worms inside her mouth, her nose, tearing her shirt off, scraping at her skin until it's nothing but torn flaps hanging down. The wormy tendrils shooting and pulsing from Dash's mouth and eyes and ears.

His ribcage opens like two doors creaking apart. Long feathery whips emerge from his torso and stroke her skin.

Mark feels frozen in terror – the worms are wriggling, from Dash's ribcage – boring out from them, feathery, barnacle-like fans – moving swiftly, tickling her breasts and along her ribs. Her eyes are wild and the worm-appendages of the thing reach into her ears – and they are –

Mark shouts, "I have light! You have no power in the light!"

He waves the flame around, his arm outstretches, his body taut. "I'll set you on fire!"

Shivering, he walks towards what Dash has become:

A creature with huge beetle-like wings, four of them, spread wide, another layer of nearly-transparent wings in between.

Mark stands, bone in one hand, lighter in the other, the flame shooting up high.

Mark tries to read the bone, but he can't – *not while Michelle is still...*

But he tries. The symbols on the bone seem different than they did before. They seem to have smudged or moved around and he can't quite see them for the flickering light.

With the light, he can see the sores and pustules along Dash's spine.

Dash turns for a moment, his face covered with many small black eyes, and he says, his words rapid-fire and ripe with excitement, "the light doesn't matter now, Mark. Not once the incarnation has happened. All the world is white light. Once in the flesh, I'm indestructible. Unless you remember the Words. But you don't, do you? You will never read the bone, will you? How can you? Only the priests who have studied for decades can remember them, can speak them," and then the creature turns about to Michelle's beatific and glowing form, blood shining along her body, and begins devouring her like a spider feeding upon a wriggly fly caught in its web.

"Oh, so delicious, such a de*lee*cious treat," Dash says, his mouth foaming with white and red.

Then, his opening body, like a mouth, covering her, a Venus flytrap, a devourer.

Mark moves toward him and thrusts the flame against his neck, but the worms shoot out from beneath wings and tear the lighter from his fingers.

The creature turns, its face bubbling with sores, its eyes blinking in unison.

It regards Mark with some interest.

The wings close, and it floats inches downward until it touches the floor.

Then, it shoots slender tentacles around Mark's waist and chest. He presses against them, but he can't pull free.

It lifts him up, and he feels the invasive, parasitic wormy fingers moving against the holes in his ears, pressing down onto his lips, forcing them open.

Lower, his navel is stretching as the worms push inward.

Wave after wave of nausea hits him.

The slick, wet tendrils pry the sacred bone from his fingers.

What feel like bundles of worms thrust down the back of his throat.

He feels the sharp jab against his stomach –
the bone –
going into him.

DASH'S VOICE, nearly sweet, whispering along with the dreadful humming of the wings as they move rapidly. "I won't let you hurt for long, Marco. I want you and me to be together. We can do anything now. Anything, and we'll bring the Nowhere into daylight. We'll tear the Veil."

Dying? Mark wonders as pain seeps through him. Blood is pouring from his stomach and legs.

Dash, in the dark, seeming human, seeming not to have a thousand wormy tentacles and barnacle feathers, lifts Mark up.

Lifts him with two arms.

Broken bones shift. Freezing pain.

No screams left in him. Mark is sure now that he screamed the whole time that the creature slaughtered Michelle.

Through the narrow hall they go, Dash seeming human but not human, carries him like a soldier holding a beloved friend on the battlefield.

Smell of fresh air.

Outside again.

Sky, clear.

Moonlight, very little, but enough.

DASH STRIPS Mark's shirt off. With his fingernails, he scratches markings on his chest and stomach.

"You can be like this, too. Just like we said. We never have to be apart. We can be in the

Nowhere. And still here, too. Still alive. There's a way."

"No," Mark tries to lift his head, but can't. "Please, I need help, Dash."

Dash lets out what can only be a sigh of contentment.

"None of this has to change who we are. This is just the god thing. It's what gods have to do. Look, Mark, I know things now. I gained knowledge. Yeah, it hurts some, and part of me feels bad, but when it takes me over, man, you have got to experience this. It's like...like *life*. Like there's no darkness at all. There's a whole other world you can see when you're like this. You can see things without your eyes. You have feelers. You have these parts of you that can stretch out and find things without even opening your eyes.

"And them? Michelle and Danny? Shit, they're in another place. Death isn't bad for them. They're the food of the gods, that's all, They're chow. Gods eat life. That's how it goes. The god of grass eats grass and the god of the flesh eats flesh. You can't have life without this. It's something we've all gotten away from, but the worshippers, the priests of the Nowhere, they know. They kept the ritual. They put themselves at one with the gods to do this.

"*We* are anointed ones, we're gods in flesh. You can't be afraid. You can't look at this with the same eyes you had before, not once it happens. It's stupid and human of you to do it. When you die, you're not going over there. You're going to come back here. Do you know what the gods are? Do you? *Do you?*"

A hiss comes from Mark's lips as he looks up at the dark figure.

"The gods are creatures, just like us, but they don't have boundaries. They reshape themselves at will. They let their hunger loose. Their lusts. Their wants. We think things happen because we do them or there are natural laws, but Marco, there aren't natural laws – the gods make things happen, they make it all go. But their names are power. I have the power. It's within me," Dash says, passion swelling in his voice. "I can be anything, Marco. *Anything.*"

MARK, in the muddy grass, at the edge of the grave.

He looks up at what once had been Dash.

What is still Dash.

The moonlight is soft around his scalp, almost like a halo.

Dash has a beautiful face. Dash has an ugly face.

Michelle. Danny. Gone. In less than an hour.

It still looks enough like Dash, with his hair, stringy from rain, matted with mud. His longish jaw and his eyes that shine even in the absence of light.

Just two eyes. Two human eyes. No thousand eyes of some monster. Darkness around his lips. Blood?

"You're dying," Dash says. "Don't be afraid of it. Just say the names. Just say them, Marco."

"Mmm," Mark said.

"We never have to live anywhere but in the Nowhere again. Not ever," Dash says.

"You're dead," Mark whispers, but isn't sure if Dash can even hear him. Mark feels so weak, his life draining.

"The names," Dash says. "Remember? You say then as you die. The first part. I say the other half of the names after you breathe your last. I know all their names now, Marco. I know each of the gods, and their wonderful hungers and the way they look – I can see them all around us. We are their children. I have them incarnate within me, too. I can be a thousand different things. I can be a hornet or dragon, Marco. I can bring up a wind or burn with fire. I can see clearly, more clearly than I could in daylight, see with more than just these useless eyes. I can smell my sight, I can feel sight. You will, too! We can go to Rachel's party. We don't have to miss it. We can bring her the puppy. I'm not going to hurt the puppy. It's not like that. What's inside me now, it has meaning. It doesn't want puppies and turtles and goats and chickens. It wants more than that. Everyone will be there. Everyone from our class. And we'll show them that we're not just there for their pecking order and social put-downs. We'll be there to show them the faces of the gods. We could even bring some more of them back, if we're careful with their bodies. We could make all of us live forever, if you really want. I mean, yeah, it's too late for Michelle and Danny, but I let it out too much. I hadn't learned how to pull back on the reins yet. But I think I understand now.

"And the Nowhere is with us. They think I'm a messiah. They'll know you as my lieutenant. We'll change everything. Everything in one night if we have to. We'll pull back the Veil. You and me, both. After you say the name. And then you'll be here again. We can fly, now. We can swim under water for hours. We can turn to liquid, or move within the bark of a tree. We can become the darkness. Or light.

"It'll be you and me. Brothers. Everything we are to each other will matter. In the Nowhere. We'll be gods *here*, Marco. We'll do things we couldn't have imagined before. Before it was just a game. Now, it's real. *We're* real. And the others? The people in the world, your mother and father and mine and the teachers at the Gardner School, they're the unreal ones. We can go on to Rachel's next. Just the names. Let me whisper them to you."

Mark closes his eyes.

Soft rain falling. Just drips of it. On his face.

Cooling rain.

The feeling of Dash's wet slippery hand touching his face.

"The names," Dash says, as gentle as the rain. "Just say one of them for me. I love you so much. Just say it."

Dash may have tears in his eyes or perhaps it is the raindrops falling gently on Mark's face.

OPENS HIS EYES.

The shadow of Dash's face is all he sees. The smell of his breath – the same stink of the dead body, its flesh torn open.

Mark mutters something.

"Marco?" Dash leans closer.

Mark says it as loud as he can. It comes out a whisper. "You. Not my brother. I don't love you. I don't want to be with you after I die…far away from you."

All his energy in those words. He feels smug. Numb and smug. A worm of pain somewhere in his gut, but otherwise, he's ready to go. Into the arms of Death.

Mark wants to close himself up.

To die without remembering the names.

DASH IS HOLDING HIM NOW, cradling him, practically kissing his ear as he begins to whisper something that Mark can't quite make out.

Dying. Please take me, God. Take me now.

Break me out of life. Crush my spirit and body and slam me into another place. Or just cut off whatever it is that life is within me. Keep me from the Nowhere.

But even as he dies, without wanting to, without desiring this, Mark parts his lips.

No! something within him fights against it. *Don't say it. Don't say the names!*

But his flesh is at war with his heart, and he realizes that Dash's remark had been true: *the flesh remembers.*

Mark utters the unspeakable names of the gods of the Nowhere, of the Veil. Like the worst profanity coming from his tongue.

Permission to be called back.

He cannot remember the Words that would stop this.

Only the names to begin it.

HIS LIFE SLIPS AWAY, just as if it were dropping into a pool. A rock in water, hitting the surface and slipping down into the murky depths.

He's angry as he goes down to a place where the lights dim and flash and dim.

The lights are nearly out.

He can't even sense that he is breathing or whether is holding him or not.

Dash sings some painful song in an unknown tongue as if he'd been singing it his whole life.

Mark has a sense of the others that are there –
the priests and believers of the Nowhere.

Standing in a circle around them both.

The part of Mark that still has a speck of
thought and life feels terror and calm all at once,
knowing that after he goes, that thing that Dash
has become will hold him in his arms and intone
the other part of the names, the response – the
litany – until Mark's eyes, once again, open.

8

THE PARTY

An hour or so later and several miles away, a girl of nineteen – her arms around a boy of roughly the same age – says, "Oh my god."

The lights in the house go out.

The boy kisses her again, his breath all beer. "Rachel, you know what? I hope we spend every night together this summer. Our last summer together."

"Damn, I'm not even sure where the fuse box is," the girl says, pushing her boyfriend away.

"It's a brown-out," another girl says. "They'll come back on."

"Where the hell's my beer?" a boy whines just before he begins cursing.

"Lights!" someone shouts, laughing. "Somebody hit the lights so Jack can find his beer."

"What happened to the music?"

"Party must be over. Nice hint, Rachel."

"Yeah, you want us to leave you can just ask us."

"It must be the storm," somebody says, drunken slur to his voice.

"Looks like somebody forgot to pay the bill."

"It must've been the storm."

"Yeah, or a burglar."

"I love it in the dark. There's more to kiss."

"Perv!"

"Got a flashlight?"

"Yeah. We all do."

A cell phone light comes up. Then, another.

"Jesus, it's nearly two. I better get home."

A half-dozen more lights comes up as phones are drawn from pockets.

"We've got a bunch of candles under the sink," Rachel says.

"Get your hands off me, Josh. And go get me some more beer."

"Somebody's knocking at the door."

"No, something hit the window. That a seagull? What the hell *was* that?"

"A bird. A bird hit the window."

"No, it's the front door."

"Come in!" a boy shouts.

"Where are those candles?"

"The kitchen," Rachel says. "Under the sink. Should be maybe six of them."

"You get the candles, I can light 'em up," some boy says.

He flicks on a lighter.

For a second, the small blue-yellow flame lights his face. The light-dappled shadows of others surround him. The phones cast eerie patches of light across wall photographs and furniture and faces, flattening all of it.

In the wide mirror on the back wall the reflection of the light reveals more: the enormous living room is packed.

"We need more light," someone says.

"Knock knock," a boy, a junior from the Gardner School, reaches the front door.

He draws the door inward.

A gust of steam. Humidity has risen after the rain.

Two figures in the dark, on the front porch.

"You're late," the boy says, sleepily, not quite recognizing them in the dark but thinking one of them is a geeky kid he saw once with his older sister even though he can't quite see the two guys on the porch all that well.

Can't quite remember that kid's name. Mark something. Or Matt? Marty?

"Party's almost over," the boy says.

For a split second, the boy who opened the door has an instinct but ignores it.

He thinks he should shut the door and lock it.

He hears a strange fluttering like the beating of wings of some large bird flying just above his head.

The boy takes a few steps backward as two dark figures cross the threshold and move toward him.

AND THEN, it begins.

ALSO BY DOUGLAS CLEGG

Click here to discover more fiction by Douglas Clegg.

STAND-ALONE NOVELS

Afterlife

Breeder

The Children's Hour

Dark of the Eye

Goat Dance

The Halloween Man

The Hour Before Dark

Mr. Darkness

Naomi

Neverland

You Come When I Call You

NOVELLAS & SHORT NOVELS

The Attraction

The Dark Game (Two Novelettes)

Dinner with the Cannibal Sisters

Isis

The Necromancer

Purity

The Words

SERIES

THE HARROW SERIES

Nightmare House, Book 1

Mischief, Book 2

The Infinite, Book 3

The Abandoned, Book 4

The Necromancer (Prequel Novella)

Isis(Prequel Novella)

THE CRIMINALLY INSANE SERIES

Bad Karma, Book 1

Red Angel, Book 2

Night Cage, Book 3

THE VAMPYRICON TRILOGY

The Priest of Blood, Book 1

The Lady of Serpents, Book 2

The Queen of Wolves, Book 3

THE CHRONICLES OF MORDRED

Mordred, Bastard Son (Book 1)

Mordred, Dragon Prince (Book 2)

COLLECTIONS

Lights Out: Collected Stories

Night Asylum

The Nightmare Chronicles

Wild Things

The Poisoner's Garden & Others

BOX SET BUNDLES

Bad Places (3 Novels)

Coming of Age (3 Dark Novellas)

Dark Rooms (3 Novels)

Criminally Insane: The Series (3 Novels)

Halloween Chillers

Harrow: Three Novels (Books 1-3)

Harrow: Four Novels (Books 1-4)

Haunts (8 Novel Box Set)

Lights Out (3 Collection Box Set)

Night Towns (3 Novels)

The Vampyricon Trilogy (3 Novels)

With more new novels, novellas and stories to come.

ABOUT THE AUTHOR

Douglas Clegg is the *New York Times* bestselling and award-winning author of *Neverland, The Priest of Blood, Afterlife,* and *The Hour Before Dark,* among many other novels, novellas and stories. His first collection, *The Nightmare Chronicles,* won both the Bram Stoker Award and the International Horror Guild Award. His work has been published by Simon & Schuster, Penguin/Berkley, Signet, Dorchester, Bantam Dell Doubleday, Cemetery Dance Publications, Subterranean Press, Alkemara Press and others.

A pioneer in the ebook world, his novel *Naomi* made international news when it was launched as the world's first ebook serial in early 1999 and was called "the first major work of fiction to originate in cyberspace" by *Publisher's Weekly,* covered in *Time* magazine, *Business Week, Business 2.0, BBC Radio, NPR, USA Today* and more. His book *Purity* was the first to be published via mobile phone in the U.S. in early 2001.

He is married, and lives and writes along the coast of New England.

www.DouglasClegg.com

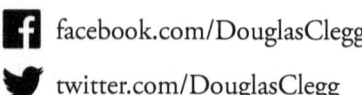 facebook.com/DouglasClegg

twitter.com/DouglasClegg

COPYRIGHT